Easter Bride

Holiday Bride Book 3

A Sweet Contemporary Romance

by

***USA Today* Bestselling Author**

SHANNA HATFIELD

Easter Bride
Holiday Brides Book 3

ISBN: 9781090871381

Shanna Hatfield
shanna@shannahatfield.com
shannahatfield.com

To the rescuers…

Books by Shanna Hatfield

FICTION

CONTEMPORARY

Holiday Brides
Valentine Bride
Summer Bride
Easter Bride

Rodeo Romance
The Christmas Cowboy
Wrestlin' Christmas
Capturing Christmas
Barreling Through Christmas
Chasing Christmas
Racing Christmas

Grass Valley Cowboys
The Cowboy's Christmas Plan
The Cowboy's Spring Romance
The Cowboy's Summer Love
The Cowboy's Autumn Fall
The Cowboy's New Heart
The Cowboy's Last Goodbye

Friendly Beasts of Faraday
Scent of Cedar
Tidings of Joy
Boughs of Holly
Wings of An Angel

Welcome to Romance
Blown Into Romance
Sleigh Bells Ring in Romance

Silverton Sweethearts
The Coffee Girl
The Christmas Crusade
Untangling Christmas

Women of Tenacity
A Prelude
Heart of Clay
Country Boy vs. City Girl
Not His Type

HISTORICAL

Pendleton Petticoats
Dacey
Lacey
Aundy
Bertie
Caterina
Millie
Ilsa
Dally
Marnie
Quinn

Baker City Brides
Tad's Treasure
Crumpets and Cowpies
Thimbles and Thistles
Corsets and Cuffs
Bobbins and Boots
Lightning and Lawmen

Hearts of the War
Garden of Her Heart
Home of Her Heart
Dream of Her Heart

Hardman Holidays
The Christmas Bargain
The Christmas Token
The Christmas Calamity
The Christmas Vow
The Christmas Quandary
The Christmas Confection
The Christmas Melody

Chapter One

Cold air that felt like it blew straight off arctic ice caps wound around Piper Peterson's neck, in place of the scarf she forgot to grab on her way out the door that morning.

The frigid sting added haste to her steps as she hurried across the back parking area at Milton's Feed & Seed to the employee entrance. The keys in her hand might as well have been shards of ice as the cold metal stung her bare hand. Fingers fumbling, she shoved a key into the lock and opened the door.

Automatically, her hand reached to the right

and flipped three switches, bathing the store with light.

"What is the deal?" she muttered to herself as she unlocked the door to the office and hung up her coat. The past two weeks the weather had been in the high forties. One day it even hit fifty-degrees. Then she awoke this morning to temperatures in the low teens, frozen stock tanks, and grumpy animals waiting for their breakfast.

She couldn't blame her collection of four-footed friends for being out of sorts. She wasn't too keen on the idea of a cold snap, either.

Piper turned on the computer in her office then put on a large pot of coffee in the front of the store so customers could enjoy it, too.

While the coffee brewed, she wandered up and down the aisles making sure the two high school students who worked the closing shift had tidied shelves, swept the floor, and cleaned the bathrooms.

Satisfied everything met her high standards, Piper walked to the front of the store and allowed her gaze to roam over the framed photographs hanging on the wall behind the cash registers. Some of the images went back to the late 1800s, when her great-great-grandfather, Randall Milton, opened the store.

Back then, the business was a livery and blacksmith shop that offered feed and tack supplies on the side. The store changed with the times, but a guarantee of friendly, honest service remained the same through all the years and generations of Milton men who'd owned and operated the store.

With no men left to carry on the tradition, her

grandfather decided to sell both the store and his home. He'd retired, hired a manager for the store, and started searching for a buyer. Four years later, he still hadn't found just the right buyer, even though he'd had plenty of offers.

Until her grandfather met a buyer he liked, Piper was proud to be in charge of the store and her grandfather's farm. If she had the money available, she'd buy both the farm and the business in a heartbeat, but that was a pipe dream. Up to the moment her grandfather turned over ownership to someone new, though, she intended to make Milton Feed & Seed the best feed store in Eastern Oregon.

She returned to the office, went through incoming emails and sent out several, reviewed the receipts from last night, and prepared the deposit to take to the bank. Those business classes Grandpa suggested she take while she was earning a veterinarian technician degree sure came in handy.

Even if she hadn't taken them, she'd spent enough summers in Holiday working at the feed store to know every detail of the business. She was grateful her father had allowed her to spend her summer vacations with Grandpa. She loved the small town and there was nothing quite like being with her grandfather. As his lone grandchild, and he her only living grandparent, they had a special bond. At least she liked to think they did. She was certain her grandfather would say the same thing.

Piper glanced at the clock on the wall above the desk, grabbed her keys, and headed to the front of the store. She unlocked the door, shoved the keys in the pocket of her jeans, and poured a cup of coffee.

Armed with it in one hand and a duster in the other, she dusted the front counter and around the merchandise on the end cap near the registers.

She turned to look behind her at the store. The center aisles held items people tended to use year-round like leather gloves, rubber boots, and tools. To the right were feed supplies, tack supplies including a few saddles made by a local craftsman, and pet supplies. To the left were racks of western and work clothing including everything from onesies for babies to cowboy boots and belts to western jewelry. She also had two aisles filled with western-themed toys, home décor, and gift items.

Piper stepped into the area that greeted customers when they walked inside the store. She liked to set up seasonal displays there. Not only did it capture their attention and garner sales, it was also a great way to call attention to the beautiful hardwood floor, original to the store. She cherished the fact it had been restored and preserved. Each time the old boards creaked beneath her boots it made her smile.

She took a deep breath, inhaling the scents of coffee, linseed oil, and leather. The store had smelled the same as long as she could remember. She never wanted it to change. There was so much history there, even if the building had been expanded to meet the needs of a growing business over the years.

The small feed and tack shop Randall started had been enlarged in the early 1920s and then completely renovated in 1940, prior to the war. When her grandfather took over the business in the early 1970s, the store was updated again. Then, just five years ago, Grandpa had given it a major facelift. From the outside, the store looked like a big, modern barn with easy-care camel-colored siding and a green metal roof. Inside, the store retained the charm and character that only an old building could offer. Many of the shelving units and display tables were antiques that had been there for decades. One big wooden hutch, with shelves and drawers, had been in use since 1901.

And she loved every square inch of it.

After another long sip of her coffee, she set the cup on the check-out counter then went to the storage room at the back of the building to retrieve a shipment that finally arrived yesterday. She'd ordered items for a Valentine display but they'd gotten misplaced in transit. It took her weeks to track down the order, but at least it arrived before Valentine's Day. She still had ten days to sell the merchandise and planned to get rid of it all.

She'd asked Hailey and Ryan, her two evening employees, to make sure the display area was empty of stock and clean so she could work on it first thing this morning. The two teens had also priced all the new merchandise, so it was ready to set out.

With a vision of exactly how she wanted the display to look, Piper hauled decorations she'd set aside to the front of the store. From the array of items tucked into boxes and storage tubs in the storeroom, she didn't think anyone in her family had ever gotten rid of anything they thought might be useful in the future. Right now, she was glad of that fact.

Groaning beneath the weight of a child-sized bright red 1950s Chevy pickup, she managed to maneuver it onto a flatbed hand-cart and haul it to the front of the store. Once there, she debated how she'd get it on the sturdy display table made of reclaimed barnwood.

If she had to lift that thing by herself, she could almost envision explaining to the doctor at the emergency room how she'd ruptured her spleen or ended up with a hernia. She ran through a list of people she could call to help, but most of them were already at work for the day. She certainly wouldn't ask Grandpa to give her a hand. Not at his age. In spite of his military bearing that came from years in the Army, his white hair and slower steps reminded her he was in his eighties.

The bell above the door jingled and Piper turned to greet the first customer of the day. Recognition broadened her smile as she welcomed a friend.

"Well, if it isn't Carson Ford. I haven't seen you since before Christmas. Did you enjoy the holiday?" she asked. "Weren't you and Fynlee expecting all your family to join you?"

The rancher made a beeline for the coffee pot set up near the cash register as she talked and poured a disposable cup full of the hot liquid.

"We had a great Christmas," he said after taking a sip of the coffee. "It's our first Christmas as a married couple and we thought it would be fun to host a big family gathering for my folks and three brothers, along with Aunt Ruth and Fynlee's grandmother at the ranch. It turned out to be a wonderful holiday. One of my brothers decided to stay."

"Oh, that's great. Is he still here?" Piper asked as she moved two smaller display tables closer to the big display table.

"He is. He wants to work on the ranch through the summer to see how he likes the area. Colton never spent much time visiting the Flying B like I did when we were kids, but he needs time away from the family ranch. This will give him a good opportunity to figure out what he wants to do with his future."

"It's nice of you to give him a place to stay and a job at the Flying B." She glanced over her shoulder at the rancher. "If he needs extra work, I'll be hiring seasonal help in a few weeks."

"I'll let him know." Carson took another drink of his coffee. "What about you? Did you and your grandfather enjoy the holidays?"

"We did, although he seemed to be pining for a certain sweet woman while she was out at your ranch." Piper shot him a teasing smile. "Grandpa is quite taken with your aunt, even if Ruth doesn't realize it."

"Oh, I think Aunt Ruth is well aware of his interest. It's what she plans to do about it where things get hazy." Carson grinned. "We all think Rand is great and she practically beams whenever his name comes up. Just give her some time. When she's ready, Rand can sweep her off her feet."

Piper laughed at the image of her grandfather playing a dashing hero at his age. Stranger things could and did happen, though. She looked back at

Carson as he took another drink of coffee. "So what brings you into town this morning?"

"With that storm we're supposed to be getting later today, I decided I better get a load of feed before it snows. I parked the pickup back by the loading dock," Carson said. He took another long drink of the coffee then held the cup up and grinned. "That sure hits the spot on a cold morning. You'd think after such a mild winter we'd be heading into spring now that it's February, instead of dreading a blizzard."

Piper nodded her head. "I'm hoping the weatherman is wrong and the storm will pass right on by, but it sure is cold out there."

"It certainly is." Carson refilled his coffee cup and leaned back against the front counter. "How's your new rescue project coming along?"

Piper smiled at him. "Charlie is doing quite well. Just yesterday, he ate a carrot right out of my hand."

"That's great, but be careful around him," Carson cautioned. "He's a big horse and I'd hate for you to get hurt out at the farm with no one around to help you."

"I am careful, but I feel bad for Charlie. His hooves are a mess. I had the local farrier come out, but he took one look at Charlie and refused to work with him. I haven't been able to find anyone who's willing to do the job."

Carson gave her a studying glance then took another sip of coffee. He tipped his head toward her. "I might know someone who could help you out. If you think Charlie can wait until this weekend, I'll see if he's available."

"I don't think a few more days will make a whole lot of difference at this point, considering everything Charlie has endured."

Piper had a soft spot for animals that was a mile wide and twice as deep. Frequently, she took in animals in need of a helping hand. Most often, she nursed them back to health then found good homes for them. Since moving to Holiday last year to take over managing her grandfather's store and keep up the house and farm until it sold, she'd slowly been collecting animals she couldn't bear to send to a new home.

Right before Christmas, she'd been driving down a back road after delivering a load of feed and saw a blue roan draft horse in a mud-bogged pasture. The Belgian, with his black mane, tail, and legs, would have been a showstopper if he wasn't coated in mud with large scabs across his sides and back. Ribs poked out, testifying to a lack of care from his owners.

Piper gave no thought to her own safety as she drove down the driveway and knocked on the door of a house in need of paint and a yard that looked like something from a horror movie with rusty junk, rolls of twisted wire, and some scary looking tools scattered around in the dirt where there had probably once been grass.

A sour-smelling man with beady little eyes and stained teeth answered the door. When she asked about the horse, he spewed a stream of tobacco that landed just shy of her foot along with a torrent of cuss words about his ex-wife that made Piper's ears ring just thinking about them.

"That ignorant horse ain't worth the feed I've been pouring into him. If you want that rotten beast you can have him!" the man yelled, then slammed the door.

Obviously he hadn't been feeding the horse and goodness only knew how the poor animal ended up covered with cuts, but she had no opportunity to question him.

Piper didn't give the man a chance to change his mind. She rushed home, hitched her pickup to her grandpa's horse trailer, and returned to the farm. Much to her surprise, the man came out with papers for a horse named Charleston Tango and signed ownership over to her. She thanked him then set about loading the big animal. It took her an hour of patient coaxing to get him inside the trailer, but she'd finally done it. On the drive to her farm, he kicked the sides and made such a racket, she thought he might end up wrecking the vehicle before she made it home and released him in a small pen by the barn.

The horse snorted and reared, and nearly kicked her in the head once before she got him fed and watered. The next morning, she had the vet come out and attempt to doctor his wounds. The vet had to give him a tranquilizer to clean him up, but the deep cuts hadn't become infected and were now well on their way to being healed. Once the blood and mud had been washed away, Piper realized she had a truly gorgeous horse in her possession.

After six weeks, she'd made great progress with Charlie, as she decided to call him, even if he still had trust issues. Who could blame him? She wanted to have the man who'd abused the animal arrested, or give him the same treatment he'd given the poor horse, but she was just glad she'd been able to rescue Charlie.

"It's a good thing you do, Piper Peterson. Not everyone would be willing to risk life and limb to save an abused animal," Carson said, giving her a smile then tossing his empty coffee cup in the trash. He pointed to the red truck on the flatbed cart. "Need some help with that?"

"Oh, do you mind?" she asked, relieved to have an offer of assistance.

"Not at all. Where do you want it?" Carson removed his coat and laid it on the counter then walked over to the truck.

"Just on this table," she said, placing her hand on the big display table beside her. "Once it's on there, I can roll it into place."

"This thing is probably worth a small fortune," he said, straining as he hefted the little pickup off the cart. Piper grabbed the back end and Carson shifted to the front. Together they set it on the table and released a collective breath of relief. "Where'd you get it?"

"Grandpa has had it for as long as I can remember. I think his dad got it in some promotion they ran when the pickup rolled off the assembly line back in the fifties."

Carson's eyebrows raised and he grinned. "And you're going to set it out here for anyone to try and steal?"

She laughed. "As you just noted, it weighs a

ton and no one is going to be able to walk off with it. Like the other vintage items on display, it isn't for sale. Everyone who works here knows if there isn't a price tag on something to ask before selling it."

"Your grandpa sure has a lot of neat antiques." Carson looked around the collection of Valentine merchandise she had piled in shopping carts and spilling out of boxes on the floor. "Valentine's display?"

"Yep. My shipment of merchandise was lost in transit but finally arrived yesterday. There's still time to sell it all." She glanced at him as she filled the back of the little pickup with heart-shaped boxes of decadent chocolates she ordered from a manufacturer in Seattle. "You wouldn't be in the market for any special Valentine's gifts, would you?"

Carson smiled. "Fynlee and I married a year ago on Valentine's Day, so I've already got a special anniversary present for her, but I haven't picked out something for a Valentine's Day gift. Any recommendations?"

Piper showed him several pieces of silver heart-shaped jewelry she'd just gotten in, suggested a few ideas based on what she knew about his wife, and offered to gift wrap his selections when she tallied up his bill for the feed.

"It will just take me a minute to wrap this up. Do you prefer pink or red paper?" she asked, picking up his gift selections.

"Definitely red for my Rosie Red." At her questioning glance, he grinned. "That's my nickname for Fynlee."

"That's so sweet. Red it is."

She turned away from the front counter to a long plank shelf attached to the wall behind it where there were rolls of wrapping paper and spools of ribbon. When she'd been moving things around in the storage room last week, she'd found a new roll of pink paper with little pastel flowers that would work through Easter along with half a roll of red paper dotted with tiny white hearts. After she wrapped the box holding Carson's gift for his wife, she tied it with a white ribbon and fastened on a red silk rosebud.

"Here you go," she said, handing the box to the rancher.

"That looks really nice, Piper. Thank you." Carson took the box and started for the door, then snapped his fingers and turned back around. "I better get something for Aunt Ruth and Grams while I'm at it."

"Of course. What do you think they'd enjoy?" she asked, pulling more merchandise from boxes on the floor to show him.

Carson made his selections, waited while she wrapped the gifts, then took the paper shopping bag she handed to him with his purchases.

"Thanks, Piper," he said, heading toward the door.

"Thank you for your help and spending your money here this morning," she said with a grin. "Tell Fynlee I said hello."

Carson nodded. "Will do. And if the person I know is willing to take a look at Charlie, I'll send him out to see you Saturday morning."

"Great! I sure appreciate it, Carson. Stay warm out there."

He raised a hand in a departing wave before he stepped out into the cold and the door shut behind him.

Piper was busy for the next hour with customers who braved the cold and came in to shop. Her assistant manager, Jason, arrived at ten and took over waiting on customers while Piper tackled the Valentine's Day display. When she finished, she stepped back and gave it a critical eye. In addition to the red truck with a bed full of candy boxes, she'd placed red, white, and black metal stars around, hung up a banner made of burlap with red felt hearts, and set a few red and white graniteware pieces around. She stacked little wooden signs with love sayings, red and pink candles, and inexpensive pieces of jewelry on a tiered metal stand. Red and white painted mason jars left from Christmas now had jute tied around the tops with pink ribbon roses and hearts glued to the string.

Jason helped her carry two mannequins to the display area and she dressed them in dark jeans with red shirts. The male mannequin wore a black vest with a black wild rag around his neck while the female had on a cream sweater with a fluffy cream-colored scarf. After setting cowboy hats on the heads and dangling a leather bag bedazzled with a rhinestone heart from the female mannequin's hand, she tucked more candles and red, white and pink items, like boot socks and gloves, into the display. To finish the presentation, she wrote "Shop in the

Name of Love," on a chalkboard and placed it front and center where anyone entering the store was sure to see it.

The bell on the door jingled and she looked back at the customer with a happy smile.

"What do you think, Grandpa?" she asked as Rand Milton made his way to her side and studied the display she'd created.

"Festive. Fun. I like it, honey." Rand wrapped an arm around her shoulders and gave them a squeeze. "You're doing a great job with the store. I'm so happy to have you working as the manager. When Lydia let me know she was moving to be closer to her son and his family in Spokane, I wasn't sure what I'd do. She'd been the manager since I retired. Thank goodness, you were willing to help me out."

"I love being here in Holiday, Grandpa. You know there's nowhere else I'd rather be. Besides, managing the store is fun for me, not work."

"I know, honey, and that's why I'm thrilled you're here. The store hasn't looked this good or had such steady sales in years." Rand gave her another hug then went to get a cup of coffee.

Once he'd taken a long drink, she motioned for him to follow her to the boot section where they could sit and visit a moment.

"What are you doing out on such a cold day, Grandpa?" she asked as she leaned back in one of the chairs people sat in to try on boots, doing her best to ignore the mess someone had made in the children's boots section.

"I heard it's gonna snow and thought I'd get

out and around while I still could. I hate being cooped up inside." He glanced at her. "Guess you inherited that from me."

She smiled at him. "I sure did. Mom never enjoyed the great outdoors all that much, at least from what I remember."

A wistful look passed over his face. For a moment, he seemed lost in memories of his only child who'd died from ovarian cancer far too young. "Your mother was always trying to be a little lady. She loved to throw tea parties for her dolls and friends. I think you get your talents at doing crafty things and decorating from her, even if you've always been a tomboy at heart."

Thoughts of her mother, how much she missed her, made Piper's heart ache, so she abruptly changed the subject. "Carson Ford was in this morning. He mentioned one of his brothers decided to stay at the Flying B for a while. Have you met him?"

"The brother?" Rand asked with a teasing smile. "Why? You interested in him? I thought I heard you had a date Friday night with the Guthry boy. If you don't get busy and find a husband, how can I hold onto my hope of having a great-grandchild to cuddle someday?"

"I did go out with Grady Guthry, but we're just friends, so don't go picking out colors for a nursery." She scowled at her grandfather. "Just to clarify, I'm not interested in Carson's brother. I wondered what he was like. That's all. And if you're gonna be ornery, I'll ask you how Ruth's doing. Got a date with her yet?"

Rand glared at her. "You know very well how things with Ruth are going — nowhere. That woman… Oh, she frustrates and fascinates me so." He released an exasperated sigh.

Piper laughed. "She'll come around one of these days, Grandpa. Don't give up."

"It doesn't bother you that I'm interested in someone who isn't your grandmother?"

Piper shook her head then placed a hand on her grandfather's shoulder, giving it an affectionate pat. "Not at all. Grandma's been gone almost eight years. I think it's awesome someone caught your eye. You deserve all the happiness in the world, Grandpa."

"Thank you, honey." He leaned over and kissed her cheek. "As for Colton, that's Carson's brother, he was at church with Carson and Fynlee twice since Christmas. How did you not notice him?"

Piper shrugged, unwilling to tell her grandfather she'd been so busy watching him watch Ruth, she hadn't paid attention to anyone else.

"Colton and Carson look quite a bit alike, both tall and brawny. From what I've observed, Colton seems like a nice young man."

"How young?" Piper asked as she rose from the chair. Unable to sit idle for long, she went to work straightening the children's boot boxes.

"Oh, I'd guess him to be around your age. Ruth told me the ages of all four boys, but I've forgotten. I think Colton is next in line behind Carson." Rand pointed to an area on the far side of the store, visible through the cross aisle. "Did you order the chicks? Won't they be arriving in a few weeks?"

Piper nodded as she finished straightening the boot area. “Yep. They should arrive on the twenty-fifth. Want to show me how you usually set things up?”

“Sure.” Rand stood amidst creaks and groans, drawing out Piper’s grin. “Lead the way.”

Chapter Two

"You did what?" Colton Ford stopped moving with a fifty-pound bag of feed halfway out of the back of the pickup and glared at his brother.

"Oh, don't get your britches in a bunch," Carson said with a grin. "I told Piper that I'd see if a guy I knew would be able to take a look at her horse's hooves. They really are in bad shape, Colt. She rescued that horse before Christmas from Kyle Mangus. That guy should be in jail, again, for any number of reasons, but animal abuse is among them. He's not a nice person when he's sober and when he's drunk, which is most of the time, he gets real mean."

"I'm sorry about the horse, but you know I don't do the farrier thing anymore." Colt hefted the bag and carried it into the barn.

"Oh, come on, Colt. This is different. It's a horse in need of help. She's already called the local farrier and he left without doing the job." Carson stacked the bag of feed he carried then stepped back and stared at Colt. "Besides, when did you ever turn down the opportunity to spend time with a pretty girl?"

"You didn't say she was pretty." Colt tipped his hat back and shifted his weight to rest on one cocked hip. "How pretty?"

"Well, not nearly as gorgeous as my girl, but she has a bunch of dark brown hair, blue eyes, and a nice smile, in a Julia Roberts kind of way."

"So she has a big mouth, is that what you're saying?" Colt asked as he went back and got another bag of feed.

"A big smile, you lunkhead, and nice teeth." Carson bumped him in the shoulder as they both hefted more feedbags. "You've seen her at church a few times. She's Rand Milton's granddaughter and she manages the feed store."

"Well, considering the fact I've only been to the church and the Hokey Pokey Hotel since I've been here, I wouldn't know anything about the feed store or who works there."

"Not my fault you decided to isolate yourself here on the ranch except for the week and a half you went home to pack up your stuff and the few times you've gone into town to visit Aunt Ruth. Don't let her or Grams hear you calling Golden Skies Retirement Village the Hokey Pokey Hotel. They'll shoot us both."

Colt grinned. "I'll tattle that you're the one who came up with the name. I heard Justin and Sage call it that, too, when they came over for dinner last Saturday." He brushed off his gloves and closed the door on the storage room where they kept the feed. "As for Rand's granddaughter, if she was at church, I didn't see her. I was too busy watching that old codger make calf eyes at Aunt Ruth and her pretending not to notice. How long do you think she'll keep him dangling?"

"I don't know, but at their age, I hope she doesn't string it out too long. I think she feels guilty about being interested in someone since Uncle Bob has only been gone two years."

"I'm sure that's a big part of it," Colt agreed. "I also think our sweet auntie doesn't ever rush into anything."

"Unless Grams is dragging her along for the ride," Carson said, slapping Colt on the back. "I swear those two old women can get into more trouble than a whole bus load of first-graders on a sugar high."

Colt chuckled. "They do seem to have their fingers poking into a lot of pies. What made them decide they should go into the matchmaking business?"

"I assume that derived from their attempts at getting me together with Fynlee. What they don't realize is that I fell in love with my beautiful wife the first time we met, even if it took me a while to realize it." Carson climbed in the pickup and started it while Colt slid in on the passenger side.

"I hope they don't get any bright ideas about setting me up. I'm just here until I figure out what to do with my future, not take on a bride." In truth, Colt was deeply grateful his brother had invited him to stay at the Flying B.

After going to farrier school and doing quite well at it along with a horse training business he'd started when he was thirteen, he'd grown weary of dealing with city people who bought a horse and expected it to behave better than a lazy lap dog when they only rode it once or twice a year. Those people were demanding, often rude, and had no idea what they were doing. Frustrated by seeing client after client with the same scenario of ignoring a horse until something jarred their memory that they even owned one, then acting irritated when it didn't behave exactly as they expected, he quit the business and went back to working with his dad and brothers on the family ranch.

Colt had always loved horses and dreamed of working with them full-time. However, his dad was focused on cattle and didn't have time, or a place, for Colt to pursue his goals of breeding and training registered Quarter Horses.

Like Carson, he knew their oldest brother would someday take over the ranch. Colt wasn't really needed there, anyway. He felt like the last year he'd just been killing time until something else came along.

Then, when his family had all traveled to the Flying B for Christmas and Carson invited him to stay, he'd jumped at the opportunity. Carson claimed he could use the help, but even if he didn't need it, Colt was ready for a change of scenery. He hoped the time spent away from his family and their ranch near Portland would give him a fresh perspective on what it was he wanted to do with his life.

In a perfect world, he'd find a place with about a hundred acres where he could start raising quality horses and training them. But building up a business like that was a big investment and he just didn't have the funds. Sure, he'd saved up money, but it would be awhile before he had enough to buy a place and put in the type of barns and outbuildings he envisioned, not to mention acquiring quality horses.

However, he owned five horses he hoped would be the beginning of his future business. Graciously, Carson had helped him haul the horses to the Flying B. Four of them Colt had raised himself and he'd had Birdie, a sweet mare, since he was sixteen. She'd been a rescue horse he'd talked his folks into letting him bring home.

Thoughts of a horse who'd endured abuse like Birdie made him glance across the cab of the pickup at his brother. "Tell me more about this horse you want me to see."

After Carson described what he knew about the horse, it sounded like the animal was wary of humans, but not out of control.

"If you decide you can't handle him, you don't

have to work on Charlie," Carson said as he parked the pickup beneath the carport next to the house.

"Who names a horse Charlie, anyway?" Colt asked as they got out and made their way into the house for lunch.

"I think he had that name when Piper got him. Just keep an open mind will you, bro, about the girl and the horse?" Carson kicked off his boots and hung his hat on a peg by the back door.

Colt shook his head as he shrugged out of his coat. "Horse, yes. Girl, maybe."

Chapter Three

Colt wished he could forget his promise to visit Piper Peterson's horse. It had snowed an inch the other day, but the temperature hadn't crept above twenty degrees since then. Snuggled into the warm, soft covers in his bed on Saturday morning, he didn't relish the thought of spending hours out in the cold with a horse that would most likely try to kick the living daylights right out of him.

Then again, he'd given his word to Carson he'd at least drive over to Millcreek Acres and check out

Charlie, and maybe his owner.

He sighed and placed his hands behind his head as he stared up at the ceiling in his room. Dawn wouldn't arrive for another few hours, but he liked this quiet time of morning when the world was still asleep. If it wasn't so cold outside, he'd have already been out in the barn doing chores. It rarely got this nippy in the Portland area and he hadn't expected it to be quite so frigid in Holiday, either. Carson warned him they could get freezing temps and snow well into March, if Mother Nature decided to be fickle.

Colt hoped that wasn't the case.

Regardless of the weather, though, he couldn't help but wonder about a woman named Piper who went around collecting abused animals like she was picking up pop cans with a highway clean-up crew. According to what Fynlee and Carson shared, she had a way with animals and a soft spot that stretched for miles for any living thing in need of help.

Would she really be as pretty as Carson led him to believe? He rather hoped she would be. Other than the retirees at the Hokey Pokey Hotel and the few women he'd seen at church, he hadn't been around too many people since he moved to the Flying B.

The last date he'd had was to a harvest dinner back in October. The girl was a sister to his younger brother's current girlfriend, so it didn't really seem like a date to him. Actually, he felt more like he'd been asked along to keep the sister from bugging his brother and that wasn't his idea of a good time.

Colt was ready for a fresh start and maybe that meant going on a date with a pretty girl named Piper.

Hopefully, he'd be able to help her horse, too. He hated to think about what sort of shape the poor animal was in after being neglected and abused. If the job was beyond his skill to handle, he at least knew a few people he could call for advice.

Colt stretched then tossed back the covers and hurried to dress. He liked to sleep in a cold bedroom, so he'd closed the vent to the room and shut the door to the rest of the house each night. It was nice for sleeping, all cozied into his warm blankets, but getting up in the morning made him move quickly to a warmer part of the house.

After making his bed he headed downstairs and put on a pot of coffee. While it brewed, he went to sit by the fireplace in the living room with a book he'd started reading a few days ago. He clicked on the lamp beside a comfy chair and settled in.

The mystery was intriguing although he was fairly certain he'd figured out the killer. He'd just reached an exciting part in the story when a hand reached through the darkness around him and touched his shoulder. He jumped, tossing the book in the air and barely suppressing a startled yelp. A glance over his shoulder confirmed the jokester was his brother.

"I ought to clean your clock!" he growled, getting to his feet and willing his racing heart to settle back into a regular beat.

Carson chuckled and picked up the book that had fallen on the floor. "Serves you right for sitting here absorbed in a scary story." He handed the book back to Colt. "Where'd you get that?"

"From Matilda. She said it would keep me on the edge of my seat."

"Guess she was right," Carson said with a smirk then wandered into the kitchen. The coffee was ready, so he poured two cups and handed one to Colt. "Do you want me to go with you to Millcreek Acres?"

"Nah, I'll be fine on my own. Besides, if you aren't there bugging me, I might even be able to see if this Piper is as amazing as you and Fynlee claim her to be." '

"If you'd rather, I could sic Grams and Aunt Ruth on getting the two of you together. One well-placed word and…"

Colt held up his hand. "Don't even think about it or I'll do something like switch your toothpaste out with denture cream. I saw a tube of it in the bathroom Aunt Ruth uses when she stays here."

"Hey, now! You better not be messing with the person putting a roof over your head." Carson gave him a warning look.

Colt grinned. "I wouldn't think of doing anything to my sweet sister-in-law. Fynlee is fabulous. In fact, if you two ever split up, Mom said she gets to keep Fynlee and you are out of luck."

Carson scowled at him. "We aren't ever going to split up and that's a stupid thing to say, anyway. Besides, if she had to spend more than a few hours around all the Ford men at once, she'd run for the hills."

"Our prevalent cavedweller tendencies do have

that affect on women." Colt took a long drink of his coffee then reached for his chore coat. "I wouldn't really give you denture cream, but I might switch your toothpaste out for a tube of hem…"

"Don't say it!" Carson warned as he gave him a playful shove and they finished pulling on their outerwear to start the morning chores. When they stepped outside, it was a shock to discover the temperature had climbed to almost forty. The weather hinted at the promise of a pleasant day.

An hour and a half later, the two men returned to the house just as Fynlee set a stack of waffles on the table next to a plate piled with crispy strips of bacon. Orange juice, a bowl of sliced strawberries, and fluffy scrambled eggs rounded out the meal.

"This looks delicious, Fynlee. Thank you," Colt said as he washed his hands.

Fynlee's squeal drew his gaze around to her as Carson stuck cold hands down the neck of her shirt. He grinned as she tried to squirm away.

A jolt of longing mixed with a bit of jealousy shot through Colt. He wanted what his brother had found with Fynlee — friendship, companionship, and abiding love. It warmed his heart to see them so happy and in love.

Quickly drying his hands, he refilled their cups with coffee and set them on the table as Carson washed up and Fynlee carried over a bowl of whipped cream and a pitcher of warm maple syrup.

"Would you like me to go with you this morning, Colton?" Fynlee inquired after Carson asked a blessing on the meal and their day.

"No, that's okay. I'm sure you have a lot of

things to take care of since this is your day off." He smothered a waffle with whipped cream then added a generous helping of sliced strawberries. "I don't have a problem going to meet Piper on my own."

"Well, I just want you to…" Fynlee stopped and appeared to consider what she wanted to say before she continued. "Piper isn't like the average girl you might run into back home. She's…"

"Unique," Carson said, then stuffed a crispy piece of bacon in his mouth.

"Unique?" Colt asked, looking from Carson to Fynlee and back to his brother. "What's that supposed to mean?"

"Just that she is unlike anyone you're likely to meet." Carson pointed his fork at him. "And she's pretty."

"You've both mentioned that. More than once. In fact, you've mentioned it so many times, I'm beginning to think she's got to be so homely pigeons wouldn't roost on her if she was a post, dumb as a box of rocks, or just outright strange."

"None of the above," Fynlee said with a sweet smile. She turned to Carson in an obvious attempt to change the subject. "Did Aunt Ruth mention anything to you about hosting a President's Day party at HPH?"

"HPH?" Colt asked. "Where's that?"

"Hokey Pokey Hotel," Fynlee explained. "Sage shortened it to initials so she wouldn't giggle every time we talk about it."

Colt thought Fynlee's friend Sage was a lot of fun, if not a bit serious, but then he supposed that came from her having the sole responsibility of her brother at such a young age. She was just eighteen and Shane seven when she received guardianship and took over raising him. Last year, she'd married Justin James, an electrician in Holiday, although she continued to work as the receptionist at Golden Skies. Her position there guaranteed she got all the good gossip about the residents and a lot of what was happening in town.

"So what's this about a party? Your grandmother isn't going to try and dress up like George Washington or Abe Lincoln is she?" Carson asked as he helped himself to a second waffle.

"You ought to know without asking that I have no control over what Matilda Dale decides to do. She might come dressed as a cherry tree for all I know," Fynlee said as she drizzled syrup over a waffle. "Ruth mentioned she'd like us all to attend the party."

"Is it a costume party?" Colt asked.

"No, it's just that Grams, well, she…" Fynlee sighed. "She most likely will wear something eye-catching."

"I see." Even from the short time he'd known Fynlee's grandmother, he realized Matilda Dale marched to her own brass band.

Colt finished his breakfast then went out to help Carson with a few chores before he checked the farrier kit he kept in his pickup to make sure he had everything he might need to work on Piper's horse. He considered taking a shower and changing, but if he was going to trim a horse's hooves, he'd just get all dirty anyway, especially since the sun had already melted the remaining snow and turned the ground to mud.

Before Carson or Fynlee could ask him if he wanted them to go along again, he got in his pickup and left.

He switched the radio from news to a country station he liked then drummed a beat on his steering wheel as he drove toward Holiday. Carson said Millcreek Acres was located about a half-mile out of town, behind the feed store. From what his brother said, the feed store sat on the edge of Rand Milton's property, which made sense.

Colt took a right turn off the highway onto a side road then turned left at an old metal sign that said Millcreek.

Although Colt hadn't actually spoken to Piper himself, Carson told her to expect him to arrive around ten. A glance at the radio clock confirmed he was on time.

His eyes widened at the sight of a Cape Cod style home complete with three dormers and a long porch that stretched around both sides of the house. He wondered if the place was old and painstakingly restored or a new build made to look like an older property. Either way, it was a beautiful house.

Rather than stop there, he continued on to a huge barn unlike any he'd seen. Painted white with green trim that matched the house, the center of the barn was completely round. The structure stood three stories high with a small widow's walk and cupola at the very center. Flanking each side of the center section were two-story tall wings. The door to the wing on the left was open and he could see stalls inside.

Eager to explore the barn, he parked the pickup and got out, then took a moment to look around at the various outbuildings that appeared to be in good shape. An unattached garage and a small shed he assumed might be used for garden equipment were near the back of the house. A hay shed, a granary, what looked like an old cinderblock milk barn, an equipment shed, and several other buildings scattered around the immediate area. He could see pens and pastures of varying sizes then a big pasture that ran up toward the back of the feed store in the distance.

A noise drew his attention from studying the buildings to behind the barn. He walked around the corner and stopped as a woman's voice shouted from what was clearly a pen for pigs.

"Simba! I've had about enough of this," she scolded. "You know better than to get into Moe's pen."

There were grunts and bleating sounds that had to come from a goat. Colt was far enough away, all he could see was a muddy pen with mud-colored shapes moving around inside.

He took a few steps toward the pen but stopped when a dog the size of a small pony trotted from behind a horse trailer and stared at him. Although mud-splattered, the dog's coat was a rich shade of caramel brown. Heavy bones, thick muscles, and the biggest head he'd ever seen on a canine gave the animal a look of power. An undershot jaw, like a bulldog, and a furrowed brow couldn't hide the dog's intelligence even if he had paws the size of bread plates.

Expressive blue eyes sized him up. Afraid to move lest the dog decided to attack, Colt stood absolutely still. When the canine wagged his tail and offered a friendly woof, Colt released the breath he hadn't even realized he'd been holding.

"Oh, shoot," he heard the woman say. Colt glanced over to see her head pop into view before she released a startled squeal followed by a loud splat as she disappeared again. The goat bleated and the pig joined in the chorus with a series of grunts.

He started toward the woman, the big dog beside him, but before he reached the pen, she stood upright and stepped over the fence. Covered in oozing mud from the top of her head to the tips of her boots, the woman carried what looked like a half-grown goat in her arms.

Carson had assured him Piper was a beauty, but he couldn't envision it with her wearing baggy, filthy coveralls and muck smeared all over her hair and face. At this point, he wasn't sure he wanted to find out more about a female who appeared unfazed by the fact she dripped a trail of oozing, rank mud as she strode toward him.

"Hi, there! You must be Carson's brother. I'm Piper."

She walked right up to him and Colt had to battle the urge to wrinkle his nose at the smell of goat and pig that filled the air around her. Normally, that kind of stuff never bothered him, but the overpowering odor made his stomach churn. Maybe he was coming down with something.

"Let me put Simba back in his pen and then I'll show you Charlie." Without waiting for his response, she marched over to an enclosure that looked like a small fortress with a high fence running around it. A covered area at the back provided a place for the goat to get out of the weather. Despite the secure lodging, he had an idea Simba had mastered the art of escaping.

Dumbfounded by the woman who didn't seem at all disturbed by the fact she'd literally been wallowing with a pig to capture a goat on the lam, he remained rooted to the ground, waiting for her to return.

"I see you met Doogie," she said as she walked past him and tugged up on the handle of a freeze faucet located at the end of the barn. She thrust her hands into the stream of icy cold water and washed them off then swiped at the muck on her face, managing to wash away some of it before she shut off the faucet. A red bandana she pulled from her back pocket served as a towel. Without wasting any movements, she hastily dried her hands then dabbed at her face.

"What is he?" Colt asked, still so befuddled, he could hardly think straight.

"A *Dogue de Bordeaux*, also known as a French mastiff," she said, nodding toward the dog. "When I found him, he had a broken leg and had been nearly starved to death, but he's doing just fine now. Aren't you boy?"

The dog gazed at the woman with such a look of adoration, no one could have questioned his affection for his rescuer.

"He looks like the dog from that old Tom Hanks movie," Colt finally said.

"Yep. Same breed. I think Doogie likes you." She smiled, showing off teeth that gleamed white against her dirty face. Carson hadn't exaggerated about her having a big smile. In spite of himself, Colt thought it was a nice smile, friendly and warm.

Tentatively, he held out his hand and let the dog sniff it then reached out to pet him. When the big canine leaned against him, Colt grinned and scratched Doogie behind his ears.

"Now you've made a friend for life." She started toward a side door on the barn. "Come on, I'll show you Charlie. I've got him in a stall since I thought that would make it easier to take a look at him."

Colt mutely followed her inside the barn, admiring the fine construction, the clean and tidy appearance, and the giant Belgian draft horse with his head leaning over the door of a stall.

"That's Charlie?" he asked, slowly approaching the massive horse.

"Charleston Tango, but I call him Charlie. I'm not sure what his previous owners called him." Piper reached up and rubbed her hand along the horse's neck. If the animal could purr, Colt thought he might have started the moment she touched him.

"He's not nearly as tough as he likes everyone to think," she said in a soft voice that made something tingle along the back of Colt's neck.

There was no way he could be interested in a woman who looked and smelled like she'd crawled through a drainage pipe used for sewage. In fact, Colt couldn't think of a woman he'd ever met who'd so unabashedly stand there in such a state.

He wasn't sure he knew one who'd have gotten that dirty in the first place. Well, Fynlee might have, but only if absolutely necessary, not that Carson would ever put her in a position for the need to arise.

Colt stepped behind Piper, ignoring the stout pig and goat odors as he gave the horse a moment to get used to him being there. He peered over the stall door down at Charlie's hooves. They really were in bad shape. Not the worst he'd ever seen or handled, but the horse definitely needed some help.

"I'll do the work, but what's his temperament like?" Colt moved back and glanced at the woman as she continued rubbing and scratching the horse. Charlie seemed completely relaxed.

"He tried to kick me a few times the first day he was here, but once he realized I wanted to help him and not hurt him, he settled right down. I haven't had a bit of trouble with him since then. He's a good boy, and sweet, but I'm not sure how he'll take to a man touching him." She glanced at him over her shoulder then turned back to the horse. "If we tie him in the center aisle, would that give you enough room and light to work?"

"It should," Colt said, backing toward the door. "I'll get my tools if you want to get him ready."

More than an hour later, he straightened and stretched his back after he finished the last hoof. He'd been as gentle and careful as he could be with the horse. Charlie had behaved very well, all things considered.

To her credit, Piper had stayed right there with a hand on Charlie that seemed to comfort him as Colt worked. They hadn't spoken much, but when they did, it was to the horse rather than each other. He didn't know what it was about the muck-coated woman, but she made him as nervous and uncertain as he'd felt when he was thirteen and going to his first dance at school.

"I'd like to come back in a few weeks just to check on him, if that would be okay," Colt said as he cleaned his tools and returned them to his farrier kit. He unbuckled the leather chaps he wore and rolled them up, tucking them inside with the tools.

"That would be great," Piper said, unfastening the ropes they'd tied on each side of Charlie's halter to help hold him steady. "I think we should call you a horse whisperer. You definitely got on Charlie's good side."

Colt ran a hand along Charlie's neck and gave the big roan a soft pat. "He's a nice horse, Miss Peterson. And he's lucky you made the effort to rescue him."

"I'm the lucky one to have him," she said, flashing that wide smile again as she led the horse to his stall. "And call me Piper."

Charlie took tentative steps, like he needed to grow accustomed to the new feel of his hooves, as he followed her into the stall. By his body language, Colt could easily see the horse was relaxed. When Charlie nuzzled the back of Piper's coveralls, Colt grinned. He gave the horse one more pat on the rump then stepped back so Piper could move out of the stall and close the half door.

If Charlie really wanted out, Colt doubted the gate would hold him, but he didn't think the sweet-tempered horse was the type to bust out for no reason. That seemed more like the goat's style.

He turned to Piper as he picked up his farrier kit and walked with her toward the big open doors where he'd parked his pickup just outside.

"Would you like to see the rest of the barn?" she asked as he studied the great architecture in the massive building. The entire place appeared to have been constructed by a talented craftsman, not just slapped together to make a shelter or storage area. Every piece of wood fit together perfectly. To his surprise, the wood was clean without a cobweb in sight, like someone frequently took a broom or brush to it, which seemed insane considering the size of the barn.

"I'd like that," Colt said. "I'll put this away and be right back." He hurried to place his tools in the pickup then returned to where she waited by the open doors. Doogie leaned against her right leg while two of the ugliest kittens he'd ever seen rolled around her feet. The dog sniffed the felines and licked one, leaving behind a trail of slobbers. Indignant, the kitten yowled and looked up at Piper, as though it tattled on the dog.

She laughed and picked up the half-drowned kitten, wiping away the dog's slobbers on the sleeve of her coveralls. "Poor baby. Doogie's just trying to be friends."

"What are they?" Colt asked, scooping up the other kitten and studying it. Both kittens bore coats of mottled color. Neither had tails. And their little faces looked like they'd been squished with noses that stuck out higher than they should and slightly sunken cheeks.

"Kittens, Mr. Ford. These are kittens."

He tossed Piper a chastising glance as he held up the kitten and stared at its face and form. "I know that much, but they don't look like any kittens I've ever seen."

"I'm sure they come from an assortment of breeds, and the vet had no idea what happened to their faces. Their tails are naturally bobbed. I found them in front of the dumpster at the grocery store a few weeks ago. The poor little sweethearts were so hungry. I don't think they'd had their eyes open all that long then, either. It's hard to imagine who could just abandon them like that."

The fact she'd rescued the kittens didn't surprise him in the least. That seemed like something she would do, no matter how homely the little things were. He looked over at Piper as she cuddled the kitten close.

"The horse is Charlie, the goat is Simba, the pig is Moe, and the dog is Doogie." He grinned at her. "I can't even guess what you named these two."

She smiled at him and raised her gaze, meeting his. Something in his chest started to thud as he stared into the most incredible blue eyes he'd ever seen. Carson had said they were blue, but he failed to say they were the exact same shade of blue as a robin's egg. He'd never seen anyone with eyes that particular remarkable hue. Intrigued, he took a step closer to her before he realized what he'd done.

Much to his dismay, she looked back down at the kitten she held. "This is Felix. He hates getting dirty and spends much of his day giving himself a bath. The one you're holding is Oscar. He loves to roll in the mud and doesn't care if Doogie slobbers all over him. I think that's why the dog always gives Felix a good lick."

Colt chuckled. "Any other animals?"

"Just one horse that I ride whenever I have a spare minute or two. Before you ask, her name is Jam. Grandpa had a horse named Bread so when he let me pick a name, it seemed fitting."

Colt shook his head as he grinned at her. "No other rescue animals?"

"Not at the moment." She set the kitten down then placed her hand on the dog's back, giving him a good scratch. "You never know what might need a hand next, though."

He nodded and set the kitten he held next to his brother. The two felines went back to tussling around on the barn floor.

"Come on, I'll show you the rest of the barn." Piper opened a door behind them and he admired the tack room. Saddles that went back more than a century sat on racks lining one wall. Bridles, harnesses, and ropes hung on the opposite wall while a long wooden workbench with shelves above it and drawers beneath it filled the far wall.

Colt ran his hand over a saddle that had been well used, but also well cared for.

"That belonged to my great-great-grandfather, the one that built Millcreek Acres and opened the first feed store. There's a creek about a hundred yards south of here and that's where he got the name for the place, combined with Milton."

Colt looked at her. "So Milton is the family name, but you're a Peterson."

"My mom was raised here on the farm, but she went to Oregon State to college, met my dad, and fell in love. They married a week after they graduated, moved to Seattle, and I came along a few years later."

"What does your dad do?" Colt glanced at her then looked back at the saddles. It was like a timeline of generations told through leather.

"Something techie that I don't exactly understand. He works on algorithms for a research company."

Colt grinned at her as he walked back to where she stood at the door. "Enough said. My youngest brother is into some computer analytical stuff I don't even pretend to understand. What about your mom?"

Piper's smile faded. He caught the sheen of tears welling in her eyes as she turned away from him. "Mom passed away when I was fourteen. She had ovarian cancer."

"I'm really sorry, Piper." Colt placed his hand on her shoulder and gave it a gentle squeeze, not caring what dried-up gunk got on him. "That's tough."

"It was, but Dad remarried a few years ago. Tina is only seven years older than me, but she loves Dad and he's crazy about her. Much to everyone's surprise, they're expecting a baby this summer."

"That's exciting." Colt didn't know what else to say. He couldn't imagine what it would be like if he lost either of his parents or if the remaining parent remarried and started a second family. What would it be like to have a sibling that young?

Silence fell between them as Piper led him to a door on the opposite side of the barn and opened it. He followed her inside and his jaw dropped open. It was like someone had looked into his head and created the barn of his dreams.

"Wow!" he said, moving forward and leaning his arms on the fence of an indoor arena. Seats were built into the wall behind him, like bleachers. "Did they used to have cattle or horse sales here?"

"Both," Piper said as she moved next to him. She propped a foot on the lowest rung of the fence. "They also used to hold a rodeo here years ago. I think they stopped doing that after my grandfather's brothers died in the war."

"World War II?" Colt asked, looking down at her.

"Yeah. One joined the Army and fought the Germans. The other became a Marine and battled against the Japanese, but they both were killed in action. They were quite a bit older than Grandpa." Piper sighed as though the weight of memories and family history weighed her down. She shrugged her shoulders, like she shook off maudlin thoughts, before she cleared her throat. "Grandpa tells stories about the fun he had here as a boy."

"It's an incredible facility," Colt said, tipping his head back and noticing the narrow steps that wound around the wall of the building, leading up to the cupola at the top. Again, the craftsmanship left him in awe. "Has Carson seen the barn?"

"Yeah. He spent an hour studying the construction of the steps and the widow's walk."

Piper pointed to the opening at the top of the barn. “You can go up there if you like.”

“Thanks. Maybe I’ll do that the next time I’m here.” He moved back and glanced at his watch. He didn’t really have anywhere he needed to be, but Piper didn’t know that. She certainly didn’t need to know how much her presence unsettled him.

It wasn’t that he found her attractive, not with her face coated with streaks of muck and her hair plastered to her head with drying mud smeared all over it. The smell of goat and pig still clung to her, for goodness sakes.

But something about those gorgeous blue eyes and her brilliant smile got to him. He liked the sound of her voice and the sweetness he could sense in her spirit, too. Piper was about the most fearlessly authentic person he’d ever met, and that was saying something. She didn’t seem bothered in the least by her appearance and Colt really wasn’t all that concerned with it either. It was more the shock of seeing a woman who didn’t start blushing and stammering and rushing to repair her appearance when he caught her wrangling with the goat and pig. She marched right past him like it was an everyday occurrence. With Piper, it probably could be.

His mother was as girlie and feminine as they came. He’d go so far as to say none of the girls he and his brothers had dated had been anything but typical females when it came to getting dirty.

It was something altogether different to come across an actual, real-life tomboy.

Colt followed her through the center section of

the barn as she made her way through another doorway into the other wing of the barn. There were more stalls, a storage room for feed, and some antique equipment hanging on one wall, like scythes, a three-legged stool, and a long wooden basket that appeared hand-carved.

"That stuff is so cool," he said, moving forward to take a closer look.

"The trug belonged to my great-great-grandmother. She had beautiful flower gardens, from the stories I've heard, and used to have cut flowers in the house every day through the spring and summer months."

"Trug?" Colt asked, glancing back at Piper.

"The long, flat basket. It's made for gathering flowers. She brought it with her when she moved out here to marry Grandfather Milton. Her family came to America from England not long before that."

Colt liked that she knew so much of her family history, that it seemed important to her. He didn't know much about his ancestry. Until that moment, he hadn't given it much thought.

He studied the basket along with some of the other antiques then moved toward the door. Piper kept step with him. She'd just reached for the knob to open the exterior door when the kittens got underfoot and tripped her. She started to fall, but Colt grabbed her arms and kept her upright. As he did, he caught a whiff of something that hinted of springtime flowers and sunshine as it infiltrated the other barnyard smells surrounding her.

"Thanks," Piper said in a slightly breathless

voice as she pulled away from him. She yanked the door open and hurried outside.

Colt followed her, wondering what he'd have to do to get her to speak in that soft voice again. Shivers had raced up his spine, but that was crazy. Wasn't it? Maybe he just needed to find a date. It had most likely been too long since he'd taken a girl out for an evening of fun.

He glanced at Piper and decided he'd look around at the options at church tomorrow.

"I better get going," he said, walking over to the pickup, feeling the need to escape before his brain conjured up any more loony ideas about Piper Peterson.

"What do I owe you for the work on Charlie?" she asked, starting to take a step toward the house.

"Nothing. Consider it my contribution to helping a horse in need."

She stopped and faced him. "That's kind of you, Mr. Ford. Thank you." She smiled at him but backed away from his pickup.

"Call me Colt and you're welcome."

Before he said something stupid, like inviting her to join him in town for dinner one evening, he climbed in the pickup and left.

But all the way home, he couldn't get the sight of those amazing blue eyes out of his mind.

Chapter Four

About to drop the heavy bundle in her arms, Piper heard the bell above the door jingle behind her as she stepped into the front display area at the feed store.

"Good morning," she called without looking over her shoulder. "If you need help with anything, let me know."

"I think you're the one who could use a hand," a voice spoke from behind her, sending tingles racing up her arms. She would have dropped the décor she held if Colton Ford hadn't taken the stack of items out of her arms.

She glanced up and confirmed she hadn't imagined he was an undeniably handsome cowboy. Her gaze traveled from the black hat on his head, past the sparkling hazel eyes rimmed with thick lashes, the straight nose, an incredibly kissable mouth and square chin, to his broad shoulders. She took in muscled thighs encased in a pair of blue jeans and boots that appeared to have been recently polished. Slowly, she shifted her focus back to his face.

She assumed the Ford brothers might look somewhat alike before she met Colton. However, after seeing him in person, the resemblance in the two men was unmistakable. Although Piper considered Carson and Fynlee among her friends, she'd yet to decide about Colton. It was hard to call him a friend when his mere presence made her feel like she had scrambled eggs for brains and overcooked noodles for legs.

When Colt grinned at her, she wanted to place a hand to her chest to still the pounding beat of her heart. Instead, she lifted the top item from those he held. The previous afternoon when she'd sold out of most of the Valentine's Day merchandise, she decided to make a few décor items to sell. She still had half a dozen boxes of candy, but everything else she'd had in the display was gone.

She had Ryan tear apart two pallets then she and Hailey spray painted the boards pink, white and red. Some of them they painted with the word "love." The rest, Piper took home with her and used the saw in her grandfather's shop to cut the strips into pieces that she fastened to old barnwood in the shape of a heart.

She also ran by the dollar store and bought half a dozen white picture frames along with a few other supplies. With a box full of scrap fabric that had belonged to her grandmother, she lined the frames with red and pink material. Using her limited computer skills, she printed simple text on sheets of heavy cardstock and tacked it to the fabric, leaving an inch-wide border of fabric around the square of text that said, "You hold the key to my…" Where it should have said heart, she'd cut out a heart shape, and then glued an old key tied with a red and white string on the paper. She discovered a box in the store's storage room with hundreds of old keys, which gave her the idea for the project in the first place.

It wasn't any problem to load all the things she'd made into her pickup and haul them to the store, but she hated to make multiple trips back and forth to move the items to the display, so she'd stacked them up and tried to carry them all at once. Thank goodness Colton arrived when he did or she might have dropped everything.

Although with him smiling at her, flashing the barest hint of a dimple in his right cheek, it sure made it hard for her to concentrate on her work. In fact, she was surprised to see him at all. After the embarrassing spectacle she'd made the other day when he trimmed Charlie's hooves, she doubted she'd ever see him in the store. She wasn't even sure he'd acknowledge her presence in public. Her theory might have undergone testing at church, if she hadn't missed it. Simba got out Sunday morning and ran off. It took Piper an hour to track down the goat at the neighbor's place, and that was only because Doogie seemed to know where Simba had escaped.

Regardless, the day Colt had come out to the farm, Piper had wanted to crawl in a hole and die when she looked up from the pig's pen and saw a good-looking cowboy standing near the barn.

Covered in dog slobbers, goat snot, and pig muck was not exactly how she'd envisioned greeting anyone. The small part of her given to vanity wanted to run to the house, take a shower, then return to the barn to help with Charlie. But the practical side of her triumphed, as usual, since she'd end up getting dirty helping with the horse anyway. So she'd left on her malodorous, filthy coveralls and pretended not to care that she looked and smelled like she'd been dragged by her feet through a seeping drain field.

It had taken her forty-five minutes and washing her hair twice to finally feel clean, but by that time Colton was long gone, right along with her hopes of any friendship between them.

With him standing in her store, looking like he'd walked out of a western magazine advertisement, hope for a friendship resurfaced.

Or maybe she'd just inhaled too many paint fumes the previous day. For a minute, she was sure she could see something that looked like interest in his eyes, but that couldn't be. Not with the way he practically raced away from her Saturday. Although she couldn't blame him. She would have run away from her, too.

When the kittens tripped her and he'd caught her, holding her upright, Piper wanted to sink against the pure masculine strength of him. To rest her head against that broad chest and just breathe in his decadent manly scent.

It was silly to dream of Colt being interested in someone like her. Piper wasn't delusional. She knew most guys weren't interested in a girl who didn't mind getting dirty, could change her own oil, and enjoyed playing football. When she was in high school, instead of taking classes like yearbook or music, she was out with the boys in wood shop or mechanics.

Her dad always encouraged her to do what interested her and home economics or art wasn't it. Piper had learned from her mother before she passed away how to cook, clean, and take care of a home. Additionally, her mother had been a talented interior decorator. Piper knew her flair for setting up displays was something she inherited directly from her mom.

Fashion and beauty had never been something she enjoyed. The girls who spent all their time looking in a mirror or snapping selfies, practicing alluring looks meant to tempt boys, annoyed her.

Piper was about as no-nonsense as a girl could get.

Yet, with Colton Ford smiling at her as he stood in the midst of her Valentine display, she wished she had on a pretty dress instead of jeans and boots. And that she'd done something with her sometimes unruly hair, other than combing it back into a ponytail that morning.

Piper propped the piece of barnwood with a pink heart in the center of it against a display table then reached for the rest of the pieces Colt held.

"I'll hang onto them while you set them out," he said, grinning at her.

Mesmerized by the way the right corner of his mouth kicked up slightly higher than the left, she mutely nodded her head. It wasn't until the scent of heliotrope perfume floated around her along with the sound of something tinkling like tiny bells that she realized Colt wasn't alone.

"Piper, darling! I love this display. Carson told us all about it and Rand mentioned you'd done quite a job of decorating the store. It's wonderful!" Matilda Dale gushed as she placed her hands on Piper's shoulders and squeezed. "How are you, sweetheart?"

"I'm very well, Mrs. Dale. It's nice to see you and Mrs. Beaumont." Piper smiled at Colt's aunt Ruth. "What brings you all to the store today? I have to guess you aren't in need of a pair of rubber boots or a load of feed."

Matilda laughed. "No, darling. We are shopping for Valentine's Day gifts and were told the best selection in town is right here."

"Oh, well, that's wonderful," Piper said. She didn't know if it was her grandfather's bragging, the advertisement she'd placed in the newspaper, or recommendations from friends that had driven so many people into the store to shop, but she was thrilled with the turnout.

Not only had people purchased nearly everything she had on display, they'd also bought other merchandise while they were there, like boots and coats, shirts and jeans. Yesterday, she'd put up a sign that offered shoppers ten percent off anything red or pink. She'd even sold out of red dog toys.

Piper made an effort to carry products that weren't available anywhere else in town. She knew the florist shop and the drug store both had gift merchandise and was careful to make sure she offered something different.

With her hand-crafted pieces, she could guarantee no one would find the exact same thing anywhere else in town.

"Oh, I love that sign!" Matilda said, taking one off the stack Colt held. "I'll take this. Shall I just start a pile at the register?"

"Let me take it for you, Mrs. Dale," Piper said, carrying the sign behind the front counter and placing it on the shelf where she did gift wrapping.

"We'll help you with the display," Ruth said, lifting two "key to your heart" signs from the stack Colt held. She set them on the display table near the little red pickup. The woman tipped her head to the side and studied the pickup a moment. "Oh, I remember this. Mr. Milton had it on display for Christmas several years."

"Grandpa did?" Piper asked, taking more pieces from Colt and hurriedly setting them around the display.

"No, his father. Rand would have been in high school then." Ruth brushed a hand over the pickup. "It was always fun to see this in the store."

"Did you come in often, Aunt Ruth?" Colt asked as Matilda took another sign from him and carried it over to the cash register.

"Once in a while I'd come along with your uncle." She pointed to the old Coca-Cola cooler near the door. "He'd buy me a cold bottle of Coke to drink while he picked up supplies. There used to be a cute little wooden bench right outside the door and I'd sit there, just enjoying the sunshine and the soda pop."

"There's still pop in the cooler, although it cost two dollars for a bottle instead of a nickel," Piper said, smiling at the older woman.

"Do you remember the time Rand got a double shipment of pumpkins for Halloween? He was giving them away to anyone who spent at least five dollars in the store," Matilda said with a grin. "I think we ended up with a dozen of them. Fynlee hadn't been with us long at that time and she was so excited."

"I do remember that," Ruth said, looking wistful.

Piper took the last sign from Colt and set it so anyone walking in the door could see the big red heart fastened to a barnwood square. It was definitely a statement piece.

"I want that, too," Matilda said, pointing to it.

"Are you sure?" Colt asked as he picked up the heavy board.

"Absolutely. It will look great on the wall above my desk." Matilda noticed the racks of clothes and flounced off in that direction.

"Do you still carry those nice work gloves for

women? I could use a new pair before I help Fynlee in the flower beds at the ranch this spring," Ruth said, wandering toward the gloves.

Piper walked over with her and showed her the selection of gloves in her size.

While Ruth tried them on, she went back to where Colt looked over the Valentine's Day display. "Shopping for a sweetheart?" she asked.

"Not unless you count Aunt Ruth and Matilda," he said in a whisper. "Carson told me what he got them, since I'm supposed to deliver their gifts tomorrow."

"Is Carson out of town?" Piper asked, looking around the display for something Ruth would like.

"He took Fynlee to Portland for a long weekend to celebrate their anniversary. They're staying at a swanky hotel downtown."

"That's wonderful. So you're in charge of things while they're gone?"

Colt grinned. "That's what he told me this morning." He leaned a little closer to her. "Between you, me, and the fencepost, the hands at the ranch know more about what's going on there than I do. Aunt Ruth and Matilda just need a little riding herd to keep them from getting into trouble."

"I see," Piper said, wishing he'd keep talking in that deep, husky rumble. It had turned her limbs so languid, she questioned if she might have to sit on the floor to regain her composure. Instead, she pointed to a necklace in the display. "I bet Mrs. Dale would like that."

Colt grinned and picked up the squash blossom necklace set with red stones. "Matilda will love it.

I'll take it. And you'll gift wrap it?"

"Definitely," she said, slipping the necklace into a velvet jewelry box. She hurried over to the counter, removed the price tag, then quickly wrapped the box in red paper and tied it with a bright pink bow. Normally, she would have gone with white, but for Matilda Dale, more color was always better.

"Thanks. Now for Aunt Ruth," Colt said, returning to the display.

Piper didn't see anything that brought the sweet, genteel woman to mind as they looked through the merchandise. If he'd come in earlier in the week, she had a set of stationery Ruth would have loved, but someone had already purchased the last box. Suddenly, Piper recalled a shipment of merchandise that had arrived the previous afternoon.

"I have something in the back she might like. It just arrived yesterday so I haven't had time to tag any of it. You can come take a look if you want."

"Sure," Colt said, walking with her down the long center aisle and through a door that was marked for employees only. She went through another door at the end of a short hall and into the massive warehouse area she called the storage room. A dozen boxes stacked near the door held spring items she had yet to price, but she was certain Ruth would like one of the products she'd ordered.

She dug into a smaller box piled on top and pulled out an ivory silk scarf with watercolor flowers in soft shades of pink, peach, and blue.

Spring appeared to blossom across the fabric.

"That's Aunt Ruth for sure," Colt said, gingerly fingering the scarf.

Piper couldn't help but stare at his long fingers. She'd watched his big, rough hands hold Charlie's hooves with tender care as he trimmed them. Those same hands had gently cradled her little kitten like Oscar was a prized treasure. Only a good man, a caring man, could have such powerful strength in his hands and use it so carefully.

"I'll put it in a box," she said. She found a small gift box on the shelf where she'd recently relocated all the gift-wrapping supplies. After folding the scarf into the box and securing the lid, they stepped into the hall and Colt noticed the photos lining the walls.

"Family?" he asked.

"Yes. That good-looking, cocky one there is Grandpa, if you can believe it." Piper pointed to a black and white photograph in a vintage frame. "It was taken right before he joined the Army."

Colt laughed and took a step closer. He turned to her with a wicked gleam in his eye. "Do you mind if I take this out to show Aunt Ruth?"

"Not at all." Piper took the frame off the hook on the wall and handed it to Colt. She followed him down the aisle to where Ruth was still trying to decide between a pair of pink or lavender gloves.

"Look what we found, auntie," Colt said, feigning innocence as he settled an arm around his aunt's shoulders. "You recognize this handsome devil?"

Ruth took the framed photograph in her hands

and blushed. The image of Rand Milton showed a young man, shirtless and quite buff, standing in a pair of torn Levi's and boots. A straw cowboy hat was tipped back on his head as he leaned on the fender of an old car. She traced her finger across the face of the handsome cowboy.

"Rand used to have all the girls in quite a dither," Ruth said, handing the photograph to Piper.

"If I'm not mistaken, he still has a few of you gals running in circles," Colt said with a teasing smile.

Ruth smacked him with the pair of pink gloves and he chuckled.

"Why are you assaulting that boy, Ruthie?" Matilda asked as she approached them from the clothing section with two vibrant-hued sweaters tossed over her arm.

"Because he's being far too sassy for his own good," Ruth said. She reached up and pinched Colt's cheek, giving him a warning scowl.

Matilda looped one arm around Colt's and smiled at him. "Too sassy for his good or yours?" The woman gasped when she saw the photograph. She held out her hand to Piper and took the frame, studying the image. "That Rand was sure a looker back in the day. Guess that hasn't really changed. He's still got it and if Ruthie would just loosen up a bit, it could be all hers."

The blush on Ruth's cheeks went from pink to nearly crimson. For a moment she looked like she was about to swat Matilda with the gloves she still held. Instead, she turned to Piper and handed her the gloves.

"I'd like to get those, please."

Taking pity on the woman, Piper nodded and led her toward the front of the store while Matilda giggled and Colt snickered behind them. Although Ruth's reaction was humorous, Piper would never intentionally hurt the woman's feelings.

At the cash register, she quickly wrapped the scarf Colt selected for his aunt, set it aside, and started to ring up Ruth's gloves, then stopped. "You know, Mrs. Beaumont, there's a sweater over in the clearance section you might like."

"Well, let's go have a look," Ruth said, taking the hand Piper held out to her.

Ten minutes later, Ruth left with her pink gloves, a sweater embroidered with pink roses, and a delicate gold necklace with a rosebud fastened to the center of the chain. She also had a big box of chocolates that Piper fully intended to ask her grandfather if he received as a gift for Valentine's Day.

Matilda had a cart full of merchandise by the time she checked out with everything from sweaters and socks to a jacket, two books by western authors, a sack of jellybeans, and the wooden signs.

While Colt carried their things out to his pickup and helped the women into the cab, Piper rang up his purchases and tucked them in a paper bag.

He jogged back in and handed her his credit card.

"Thanks for wrapping that stuff for me," he said, taking the card when she returned it to him.

"My pleasure. Thanks for coming in to shop. I appreciate the business."

"Carson said you had a great selection and he wasn't exaggerating." Colt picked up the bag but didn't seem in a hurry to leave. "How's Charlie getting along?"

"Good. It took him a little while to adjust to his hooves feeling different, but he's been racing around the pasture and doing really well. Thank you, again, for working on him. I appreciate it so much."

"You're welcome, Piper. Do you think…" The honking of a pickup horn interrupted them. He leaned back so he could glance out the front doors and see Matilda honking the horn. He rolled his eyes. "I guess that's my signal to go. Carson mentioned you were looking for some seasonal help. If you get short-handed, give me a call. I'd be happy to put in a few hours."

"I appreciate the offer and may take you up on it, if you're sure you'll have time."

"Carson has plenty of help at the ranch, at least for now. When we get busy with spring work that might be a different story, but I have time to spare for the next month or so." Colt took a step closer to her.

Piper had the strangest feeling he was about to ask her something important, only Matilda choose that moment to bustle back inside the store.

"I told Ruthie I was going to see what was keeping you, Colton, but I really wanted to talk to you both without her listening." Matilda cast a quick glance out to the pickup to make sure her friend hadn't followed her inside.

"What's up, Matilda?" Colt asked, his brow

wrinkling with concern.

"I'm sure you've both noticed, as has practically everyone in town, that Rand is quite enamored with Ruth. I'm sure Ruth is the only one who doesn't realize they should be together. I know for a fact Bob would want her to snatch onto whatever happiness she could find in these golden years of her life," Matilda said, fluttering her hand in the air for dramatic effect.

"Uncle Bob would want her to be happy and she does like Mr. Milton," Colt said, looking at Piper.

His smile made a delicious shiver start at her head and trail down to her toes. She had to work to bring her focus back to Matilda as the woman continued speaking.

"I'm getting quite good at this matchmaking thing, usually with Ruthie's assistance, but I think we need to work on getting her and Rand together. Will you two help me?"

Piper grinned and turned her gaze to Colt's. "I'm game. How about you?"

"Sure. I'd do anything to help Aunt Ruth." His eyes held hers even though he spoke to Matilda. "What do you want us to do?"

"Friday evening, let's get them together at the diner. Piper, you ask your grandpa to have dinner with you there. Colton, you'll invite Ruth to join you and if she offers any resistance, I'll force her to go. Then the four of you can sit at the same booth. And if you make them sit together, even better."

"That's a doable plan," Colt said, finally pulling his gaze from Piper's to nod at Matilda.

"What time are we going to meet?"

"Would six work for you both?" Matilda asked.

"That's perfect," Piper said, thinking of how much fun it would be to join Matilda in her romantic schemes.

"Wonderful!" Matilda clapped her hands, sending the bracelets she wore into a jingling, tinkling symphony. "Now, I'll head back out to the pickup so you two can go back to visiting. No rush, Colton. Take all the time you need." She patted him on the back like he was a child before she sashayed outside and climbed into the pickup with Ruth.

"It's nice of you to go along with Matilda's plans," Colt said, giving Piper another warm smile. In fact, it made her feel like she was standing next to a blazing fire.

"My pleasure. I want Grandpa to be happy and right now his happiness has a lot to do with Ruth. She's a lovely person and I think they'd be good for each other."

"I agree. Otherwise, I wouldn't get involved in one of Matilda Dale's matchmaking plans. Perhaps if we keep her focused on Aunt Ruth and your grandfather, she won't have time to terrorize anyone else."

Piper laughed. "Perhaps. I guess I'll see you Friday."

"Friday," he said and gave her a long look. "Take care and have a nice Valentine's Day."

"You, too, Colt. Have fun with your aunt and Mrs. Dale."

"Right," he said, offering her a playful wink before he hurried out the door.

Piper pressed her hand to her chest and sighed. Colton Ford was one handsome, sweet, amazing cowboy. No wonder women spent so much time primping and fussing to catch a man's eye. Right then, Piper was grateful she was at least clean and reasonably well groomed for this encounter with Colt. A good-looking, charming guy like him wouldn't give her a second glance, though. Not when he could choose any girl he wanted.

Even if she wished he would pay her a little attention, Piper knew it was best to ignore any attraction she felt for him. He wasn't planning to stay in Holiday more than a handful of months. Once Grandpa sold the farm and feed store, Piper would head off on her next adventure, too.

Nevertheless, the idea of being anywhere but Holiday, in the house where she felt at home and working in the store she loved, made her sad, so she pushed those thoughts aside.

With a smile, she picked up the beefcake photo of her grandfather and hung it back in the hallway. Maybe she'd dig out an old photo album or two and take them with her to dinner Friday. Perhaps the old images would help her grandfather's efforts in wooing the woman in whom he'd set his affection.

No matter that the date was to get Ruth and Grandpa together. Piper couldn't wait to see Colt again.

Chapter Five

"You look lovely, Aunt Ruth," Colt said as he helped her into his pickup Friday evening. He'd arrived at quarter to six and spent a few minutes visiting with Matilda before she shoved him and Ruth out the door, offering him a conspiratorial wink.

"I love my new scarf, Colton. It's perfect," Ruth said, beaming at him as she fingered the soft silk she'd wrapped around her neck. "Thank you for being so thoughtful."

"You're welcome, auntie," he said, then closed the door. He jogged around the pickup and slid behind the wheel. He'd left the vehicle running so it would stay warm for her. "Are you hungry?"

"I believe I am. The diner always has good food, even if it isn't anything fancy."

"What's your favorite thing to eat there?" Colt asked as he backed out of the parking space.

Ruth gave him a sly grin. "A big old cheeseburger with bacon, crispy tater tots, and a strawberry milkshake. Bob and I used to get those sometimes before high cholesterol and indigestion forced us to make different choices."

Colt chuckled. "Well, that burger does sound good. It must be hard to not be able to eat whatever you want. I'm sorry."

"Oh, it's just one of the joys of growing old." She reached over and patted his hand.

"Did you have a nice Valentine's Day?" he asked. At the mention of the day full of romance, his aunt's cheeks turned pink. He couldn't help but wonder what caused her to blush, but he hoped it had something to do with Rand.

She nodded. "It was nice."

"Get anything special?"

"Well, there was the lovely scarf from you and a pair of fuzzy pink slippers from Carson and Fynlee with candy stuffed in the toes. Matilda gave me a book I've been eager to read. Oh, I almost forgot. Sage brought in the most beautiful cookies for us. She said she had to beat off Justin and Shane to keep them from eating them all."

Colt grinned. "I bet she did. I had a piece of

cake she made last weekend. It was really good." He gave her a studying glance as he turned into the parking lot at the diner. He saw Piper sitting in a car with her grandfather and decided to hurry Ruth inside. If he played it right, they could force Ruth to sit next to Rand. "Did you get any other gifts or surprises?"

"Well, a gorgeous bouquet of pink roses was delivered for me along with one of those signs Piper had in her store that said something about the key to one's heart." The blush on her cheeks deepened.

"Who was it from? A secret admirer?" he asked as he pulled into the closest parking space he could find near the door and cut the ignition.

"No. I think it was Rand Milton, although the card was signed with only a flourished R. Rather arrogant of him, don't you think?"

Colt didn't answer as he hopped out and hurried around the pickup to help Ruth get out. He tucked her hand around his arm and guided her inside. "Should we sit in that booth over there?" he asked, pointing to a booth near the back.

"Yes, let's do. It will be quieter there than near the door, and not breezy. The air out there is a little nippy," she said, walking toward the booth.

He got his aunt settled into the booth and made an excuse of going to the restroom to return to the front to wait for Piper and Rand to come in. If they were going to engage in covert matchmaking activities, he really should ask Piper for her phone number.

The day he'd gone out to Millcreek Acres, he'd been so taken aback by her, he'd returned to the

Flying B and gave Carson a bad time about marriage addling his brains if he thought a girl covered in pig poop and barnyard filth was pretty. Carson told him a little dirt never hurt anyone and to reserve judgment until he saw Piper when she wasn't dripping mud from chasing the wayward goat.

Truthfully, Colt knew he shouldn't be judging anybody about anything, but it was hard not to when Carson and Fynlee had elevated his expectations about Piper. She'd been nothing like he'd envisioned or anticipated. He'd hoped they'd hit it off and maybe could enjoy going on dates while he was in the area. Goodness knew there weren't that many eligible females in the small town of Holiday.

He'd been disappointed, yet oddly intrigued by Piper's appearance after their initial meeting. Her incredible blue eyes had stayed in his thoughts, along with the sound of her voice.

Then, when he'd gone to visit Ruth and Matilda the day before Valentine's Day and they'd insisted they wanted to go to the feed store to do some shopping, he'd been completely caught off guard by the sight of Piper at the store. While Ruth and Matilda had wanted to look at a display of old advertisements that were inside a glass-fronted case on the front of the building, he'd stepped inside. Immediately, he'd noticed someone struggling to hold onto a stack of signs and picture frames. Without giving a thought to the identity of the woman, he'd taken the heavy load from her.

The moment her eyes met his, though, he knew

it was Piper. She looked nothing like he remembered from seeing her the previous Saturday, except for that brilliant smile and those gorgeous robin's egg blue peepers.

When Ruth and Matilda came into the store, he took advantage of Piper being distracted by the two women to study her. Rich, wavy brown hair pulled into a ponytail looked long and thick. Smooth skin, dotted with freckles across her slim nose. High, sculpted cheekbones. Rosy lips. And the tiniest little cleft in her chin only visible when she smiled. Her heart-shaped face was quite lovely, far more than pretty, and to think it had been hiding under all those layers of smeared mud. Without the baggy coveralls hiding her body, he could see she had a nice figure with long legs.

He'd been about to ask her on a date when Matilda interrupted them, but this was even better. He could get to know Piper while helping Aunt Ruth find a little happiness, too.

As he walked past the diner door, it opened and Piper stepped inside followed by Rand. The older man was busy holding the door for a couple entering behind them, so Colt quickly pointed in the direction of the booth where Ruth was sitting then ducked into the restroom.

He slowly washed his hands, wasting enough time for Piper and Rand to wander to the booth before he dried them and left the restroom. He got to the table just as Ruth looked up and gave Rand a surprised look.

"Well, fancy meeting you both here," Colt said, shaking Rand's hand and smiling at Piper. "Would you like to join us?"

"Oh, that would be fun, wouldn't it, Grandpa?" Piper asked enthusiastically.

Rand gave her a strange look, then nodded his head. "Certainly."

Colt held Piper's coat while she slipped it off, then she helped Rand with his. Before he quite knew what she was doing, she'd managed to nudge Rand into the booth next to Ruth. Piper slid into the booth on the other side and Colt happily sat beside her.

"Evening, folks," the waitress said, handing them laminated menus that hadn't changed in years. "What's everybody drinking tonight?"

Once she had their beverage orders, she left while the four of them studied the menus. Colt thought the burger his aunt mentioned sounded good, but he continued looking at the menu until the others set theirs down on the table.

The waitress returned with glasses of water for everyone, coffee for Rand, tea for Ruth and Piper, and a glass of cola for Colt.

With Piper sitting so close beside him, he was grateful to have the icy cold glass to hold in his hands. The unintentional brush of her leg against his sent his temperature spiraling upward. He still hadn't recovered from the jolt that rocked through him when his fingers brushed against her soft skin when he helped her remove her coat.

The beautiful, elegant woman sitting beside him looked nothing like the mud-splattered waif he'd encountered at her farm. No, the gorgeous creature smiling at his aunt could have been attending a play or an event at the country club, not just a Friday night dinner with her grandfather.

The abundance of her lush brown hair was pinned up on her head, although tendrils escaped around her face and neck, making him long to twirl one of the silky strands around his finger. Piper wore a dress that would have been perfect for a garden party. Although it was black, the long skirt bloomed with pastel flowers around the hem. Dainty little flowers scattered across the yoke and down the sheer sleeves of the full-skirted dress. She had on black heels with straps that twined around her ankles, and a fabric-covered belt that encircled a trim waist. And she smelled like springtime.

Slightly leaning her direction, he inhaled the luscious fragrance of spring blossoms and sunshine, and something uniquely her that he'd noticed even when she carried the odors of pigs and goats on her.

Rand gave him a hard glare so he shifted away from Piper, determined to make this evening about the older gent and his aunt instead of attempting to woo the woman beside him. He wondered what happened to the tomboy version of Piper. Fascinated by the many facets of her personality, he wanted to explore them all, to get to know each one.

The fact he did left him unsettled.

He doubted he'd set down roots in Holiday. The Flying B was just a place to stay until he figured out his future. However, in the short time he'd been in the area, he'd really come to like it. If he allowed his thoughts to run wild, he'd love to buy Millcreek Acres and turn it into the horse training operation he'd dreamed of running.

Thoughts of Piper being included with the deal didn't seem as off-putting as they might have a week ago. Truthfully, he liked the notion of her being there. She certainly wasn't a girl who was afraid to work hard or get her hands dirty and anyone Colt married would have to be willing to do both from time to time.

He thought of the snotty girl Carson had been dating before he met Fynlee. None of them had liked Hilary in school and she'd only gotten worse after she graduated. He couldn't picture her stepping one toe into the mud let alone wrestling a goat who'd escaped into a pigpen.

No, his brother was quite fortunate he'd screwed his head on straight and chosen a bride so well-suited for him and his life on the ranch. Colt adored Fynlee and was even glad to have Matilda as part of the family. The colorful old woman certainly added a lot of pizzazz to life. He had a hard time picturing how his soft-spoken aunt had become such close friends with Matilda, but they were as thick as thieves.

Under the guise of taking a drink from his soda, he looked at his aunt and caught her nervously twisting a spoon around and around in her fingers while sitting as far away from Rand as possible. Pressed up against the wall, it was a wonder she hadn't scrambled out of the booth in a mad escape. Amused by the visual of his aunt trying to climb over the back of the booth with the hem of her skirt dragging behind her, he almost choked on his drink.

He set down the glass and coughed, hiding his grin behind his napkin. An elbow connected with his side and he glanced at Piper. If his imagination wasn't running away with him, she'd cast him a flirty wink. Or maybe it just seemed flirty. Or she could have just had something in her eye.

Colt took another drink from his soda, trying to decipher the meaning behind Piper's wink. Rand cleared his throat and faced Ruth, raised his eyebrows at her deer-in-the-headlights look, and sighed. He shifted his attention to Piper.

"Did you sell the rest of the Valentine's Day merchandise, sweetheart?" he asked.

Piper nodded. "I did, Grandpa. There was one big box of chocolates left, so I let Hailey and Ryan share it yesterday when they came in for work. I think Ryan has a bit of a crush on Hailey because he let her pick out all her favorite pieces before he took any."

"How sweet," Ruth said, glancing at Rand then scooting even closer to the wall.

"When did you say the shipment of chicks is due to arrive, honey?" Rand asked.

"They should be here on the twenty-fifth. I ordered the same amount as last year, like you recommended." Piper smiled at Ruth. "Did I hear you used to raise chickens, Mrs. Beaumont?"

"I did have quite a bunch of chickens back in the day. The leghorns are great producers, but I liked the New Hampshire reds the best. They are strong producers, have delicious meat, and do well in both hot and cold temperatures," Ruth said, then gave Piper a shy smile. "I thought you agreed to call me Ruth."

"Yes, ma'am," Piper said. She leaned back as

the waitress arrived with their meals. For a little while, they all ate in silence.

Colt considered how this date with Rand and his aunt was quickly turning into a disaster. He didn't know what might rescue it, but he figured it was up to him to do something. "So, Mr. Milton, Piper showed me some old photos in the store the other day. How long were you in the service?"

"Call me Rand, son," the older gent said after he'd dabbed a napkin over his lips. "I was in the Army a dozen years. I enlisted when I was young enough I thought I knew everything. Both of my brothers served during World War II and were killed in action. My folks hated to see me go, but they understood."

"Were you in Vietnam?" Colt asked, studying the older man. Although Rand seemed quite gregarious and fun-loving most of the time, he had an idea he'd seen his share of hardships and darkness through the years.

"I was there. In fact, fighting in that foreign place full of hate and death and destruction is what made me decide if I survived to come back home, I wouldn't re-enlist. When I finally returned stateside, I couldn't get back here fast enough. The day I left when I was so young and full of myself, I couldn't wait to see the world and experience everything it had to offer. It didn't take too long to realize I'd had it pretty darn good right here in Holiday."

"And you met Grandma when you came back, right?" Piper asked. She gave him an encouraging look, as though she anticipated hearing a cherished story.

Rand nodded. "I met her on my way back home. I decided to take a train across country to get back here. I was sitting at the station, waiting to board, when a beautiful young girl walked up to me and thanked me for my service. People could be so hateful to the military then, you know. I told her it was my pleasure to serve and we got to talking. We sat together and talked for hours. She was supposed to get off in St. Louis to start a job as a nanny, but right before her stop, I asked her to marry me. She said yes and we wed the day after we arrived here in Holiday."

Surprised by the man's quick proposal, Colt glanced over at Piper. She had a dreamy look on her face and even Ruth looked quite enamored with the romantic story.

"Emma was my sweetheart from the day we met until the day she passed away. We had many wonderful, happy years together, especially after Lisa arrived." Rand gave Piper a warm, affectionate look. "Your mother was such a pretty baby, Piper. I always thought you looked just like her. You still do."

"Thank you, Grandpa. Mom was so lovely and always so stylish. I'm sure she was nothing like me, but it's nice of you to say that," Piper smiled at him then glanced down and brushed self-consciously at her skirt.

"I think you look so much like Lisa, Piper," Ruth said, reaching across the table and squeezing her hand. "You've got her eyes and her smile, and her zest for life."

"She must have been a truly beautiful woman,

if Piper resembles her," Colt said, as surprised as anyone that he'd spoken the words aloud.

Piper stiffened slightly and stared at him. The tension in her shoulders relaxed when she realized he was sincere. "Thank you," she said quietly.

"What about you, Aunt Ruth?" Colt asked. "How did you meet Uncle Bob?"

Ruth got a faraway look on her face. "Well, you see, I, um… well, there was this boy I liked very much. One I was sure I loved with all my heart. Much to my dismay, he got it in his head to leave and within a week he was gone. I just knew he'd never come back and moped around for weeks. My mother had no idea what to do to help me. One summer day, she declared I needed fresh air and sunshine and sent me to the neighbor's place to pick cherries. They'd hired a bunch of local kids to do the job. Instead of accepting money, I was supposed to bring home cherries for my mother to can."

Ruth appeared lost in her memories before she spoke again. "My, but they were delicious cherries." She released a soft laugh. "I think we ate more than ever made it into the buckets, but we had a grand time. One of the girls had brought along her cousin who was visiting for a few weeks. Robert Beaumont was a few years older than most of us, but he was so handsome and sweet, and very charming. He asked if he could take me to get a soda the following day. He never did go back home, but had his folks send his things. He went to work for one of the ranchers and we married a year later. Together, we built up the Flying B from a few cows and one old horse to what it is now."

Colt had a good idea who the boy was Ruth had loved before he left town without plans to come back. This was the stuff of romance novels. He looked at Piper and she offered a brief nod of her head, as though she agreed to his unspoken question. There was much more history between Ruth and Rand than anyone realized.

Well, perhaps anyone except Matilda. He wondered if Fynlee's grandmother knew about Ruth's infatuation with Rand in her younger years. He'd have to pump her for information the next time he saw her.

"Guess what I found?" Piper asked. She pulled an old yearbook out of the bag she'd set on the floor beside her and slid it across the table.

"Where on earth did you find that?" Rand asked with a grin as he flipped open the book from his senior year of high school.

Ruth forgot her aversion to getting close to Rand as she scooted near him so she could see each page as he turned it.

"Oh, look!" she exclaimed pointing to a large photograph of what appeared to be a drama production.

"You were the star of the show," Rand said, smiling at Ruth with his heart in his eyes. "If I remember correctly, the crowd gave you a standing ovation. You deserved it, too. And you looked so beautiful."

"It was a wonderful evening," Ruth said, obviously thrilled by both the memories and Rand's compliment. "Do you remember the scene when the backdrop fell over on…"

Rand and Ruth were soon happily strolling down memory lane. Colt leaned back and slid his hand beneath the table. His fingers found Piper's and he squeezed her hand.

She looked at him with a covert grin.

He mouthed, "good job," to her as they listened to Rand and Ruth talk about days long past.

They all ordered dessert and stayed for another hour and a half as Ruth and Rand visited about people who lived in town back then, families who'd come and gone, and businesses they wished had never closed.

"Remember that little ice cream shop that used to be on Main Street? Oh, they had the best ice cream sundaes," Ruth said, glancing at Rand. "You used to steal the first bite of mine every time we went there."

Rand smirked. "True, but I always let you have the cherry off my banana split."

Colt had a hundred questions he wanted to ask, but he refrained. Piper looked like she was about to burst with curiosity, but like him kept from interrupting Ruth and Rand. A few more evenings like this, and their work as matchmakers might just pay off.

Not to mention he entirely liked a reason to sit all cozied up to Miss Piper Peterson's side.

"Oh, gracious! Look at the time," Ruth said, glancing at her watch. "I don't know how it got so late."

"Time flies when you're having fun," Rand said, winking at her.

Ruth scowled and looked as though she was

ready to give him a shove so she could exit the booth. "Since neither of us are spring chickens anymore, we really should get going."

Reluctantly, Rand swung his legs around and stood then reached out a hand to Ruth. She stared at it for a moment before finally taking it and allowing him to help her out. He took her coat from Colt and held it as she slipped it on.

Colt quickly held Piper's for her. She rammed her arms in the sleeves then hurriedly snatched the yearbook off the table. As soon as Rand had tugged on his coat, she handed it to her grandfather.

"Maybe you'd like to take that with you, Grandpa. I bet Matilda would enjoy seeing some of those photos, Ruth."

"Oh, she definitely would," Ruth said, buttoning her coat and picking up her purse.

"If you two aren't opposed to it, maybe we could do this again sometime," Colt said, trying to sound innocent.

"I suppose it wouldn't hurt anything," Ruth said, giving Rand a wary glance then tipping her head toward Piper.

Colt had no idea what that meant, but Rand cleared his throat. "Yes, if no one is opposed perhaps we could meet again next week?"

"That would be fun!" Piper said, looking at Ruth. "Why don't we try the Italian place next week? I heard they have a new pasta dish that's really good."

"Great. Should we meet at six?" Colt asked.

"Yes. That works for me," Piper said, then turned to her grandfather. "Is that okay, Grandpa?"

"Of course, honey." He smiled at her then at Ruth. "Since I'm heading to Golden Skies anyway, why don't you ride with me, Ruth? I'm sure Colton wouldn't mind taking Piper home since it's on his way to the Flying B."

"Well, I don't... I um..." Ruth stammered until Rand settled a hand on her shoulder. She glared at him, but nodded her head. "Oh, that will be just fine."

"Are you sure, Aunt Ruth?" Colt asked. He couldn't think of anything he'd like more than spending additional time with Piper, but he didn't want to toss his aunt at Rand if she was truly upset about it. He got an idea her protests about Rand were half-hearted at best, especially now that he was certain they used to be sweethearts.

"I'll be fine, darling. You have a good evening and don't work too hard at the ranch tomorrow. I'll be ready for church at ten sharp Sunday. You'll still come pick me up, won't you?"

"Of course, Aunt Ruth. I'll be there to get you and Matilda, since Carson and Fynlee won't be home until Sunday evening." Colt motioned for the others to precede him out of the diner.

The air outside was frigid, so he didn't want to keep anyone lingering. "Drive safely and we'll talk soon."

"Have a nice evening, honey," Rand called to Piper as he guided Ruth to his car.

When Ruth was inside the car, Piper excitedly squeezed Colt's arm and sighed in relief. "That went even better than I hoped, although we got off to a bit of a rocky start."

"A bit?" Colt asked with a grin. "I thought Aunt Ruth might turn on her spidey powers and scale the wall just to get away from your grandpa."

Piper laughed, the sound ringing across the quiet evening and resonating in Colt's heart. He placed his hand at the small of her back and guided her to his pickup. He opened the passenger door and gave her a hand as she climbed inside then settled her skirt around her.

He shut the door and jogged around then started the pickup. "You look amazing, Piper. That's a pretty dress."

She brushed her hand along the skirt and turned to him with a pleased smile. "Thank you. I don't get many opportunities to dress up, and it's not really my thing, anyway, but I wanted to look nice for…" She hesitated and shifted her gaze from him to the window. "For this momentous event with Grandpa and Ruth."

"It was a great idea to bring that yearbook. Those old pictures and the memories they brought to mind really helped break the ice between those two." Colt backed out of the parking space and pulled onto the street. "Did you have any idea they'd dated when they were younger?"

"No. None at all. Grandpa doesn't talk much about his teen years. It's like he wants to forget anything that happened between the time he graduated from high school until he met my grandmother. I think it's so romantic how they met on a train and ended up married a few days later."

"That is a great story," Colt agreed as he turned and drove past the feed store heading out of town.

"Did your grandmother have family she left behind back east?"

Piper shook her head. "No. Her brother was killed in Vietnam and her parents died in a car accident a year before that. She was alone in the world and that's why she packed up and decided to take a job as a nanny somewhere far away from her sad memories. I don't think she ever regretted marrying Grandpa. They were always so happy together."

Colt looked over at her. "Your grandfather seems like he's probably full of fun."

"Oh, he really is. Grandpa is just…" she paused, as though she sorted through her thoughts and memories. "He's a special person full of so much life and love. I don't know what I'd do without him."

"It's obvious he adores you, too," Colt said as he drove down the lane to Millcreek Acres and parked in front of her house. "This is such a pretty place. It's wonderful your family has such deep roots here."

"The farm is my favorite place on the planet. I hate to think of someone buying it someday, but Grandpa claims he's ready to sell both the farm and the feed store." Piper sighed as she looked out the window at the house where the front porch light glowed through the darkness. "I can't picture anyone else living here and appreciating all the history that comes along with the place. It's going to be hard when he finally finds a buyer."

"Have you told him you'd like to stay here?" Colt asked as he unfastened his seatbelt.

"No. I don't want him to feel like he can't sell it because of me. I'd buy it in a minute if I had the funds, but I don't. Even if I could get a loan, I'd never be able to take on one large enough to cover both the farm and business."

Colt got out and hurried around the pickup to open her door. Doogie trotted off the porch and came over to stand at the end of the walk where a fence encircled the yard and a gate kept him from running off. If the dog really wanted out, Colt figured he could either trample the gate or jump over it, but Doogie didn't seem like he wanted to escape.

If he'd been rescued by Piper, he wouldn't want to leave either.

Before Piper slid out, Colt glanced down at the muddy ground and back at Piper's shoes. Without giving a thought to his actions, he swept her up in his arms and headed toward the gate.

"What on earth are you doing?" she asked, her voice taking on that breathy tone that made his heart kick into an accelerated beat.

"Sparing your shoes from a trip through the mud." He forced himself to look ahead and not at the woman he held. If he did, he didn't think he'd be able to keep his lips to himself. Not when she felt so good in his arms.

Piper wasn't as tall as Fynlee, but still taller than most women. And she definitely had curves in all the right places. At the moment, he could feel a few of them and they were about to short-circuit his brain.

He was still trying to reconcile the beautiful

woman in his arms to the muddy tomboy he'd first met. The two images were at such odds, he couldn't quite put them together.

Piper reached down and flipped the latch on the gate. Doogie woofed in welcome as Colt stepped onto the walk.

"I can make it from here," she said, pushing against his chest.

"But where's the fun in that?" he teased, carrying her up the front steps and carefully setting her on her feet on the mat in front of the door.

The dog brushed against them, his big tail whacking a beat on the back of Colt's legs.

Piper opened the door then looked back at him. "I had fun tonight. Thanks for suggesting we get together again. I'll make sure Grandpa is there next Friday."

"I enjoyed tonight, too, at least once Aunt Ruth quit glaring at Rand like he carried the plague." Colt stuffed his hands in his back pockets to keep from wrapping them around Piper and pulling her against him. If he did, it was a short trip to giving her a kiss and he got the idea that wasn't going to happen.

"Have a nice weekend, Colt. I'll see you at church Sunday."

Distracted by the porch light illuminating Piper from behind and shimmering through her hair, he took a step back, bumping into Doogie. He placed a hand on the dog's head to steady himself.

"I'll see you there," he said, growing more befuddled by the moment.

Piper turned like she was going in the house, then whipped around and pressed a quick kiss to his cheek.

She ran into the house and quietly closed the door.

Grinning like an idiot, Colt gave Doogie an elated pat on his back and scratched behind the big dog's ears before he jogged back to the pickup. Maybe next week he'd finagle a kiss from Piper, a real kiss, on the lips.

Chapter Six

Piper looked in the mirror and sighed. Why hadn't she paid more attention when her mom tried to teach her about clothes, makeup, and all that girlie stuff she hated? She'd always been more interested in playing ball, climbing trees, and dragging home injured animals than she'd ever been in all the things she considered stupid and far too feminine for her liking.

Only now, all that instruction she'd half-heartedly listened to didn't seem quite so stupid.

Oh, Piper could do a decent job of cleaning herself up when she had to. She could fashion her hair in four different styles, and only three of them involved braids or a ponytail. She knew what colors looked best on her and could choose clothes flattering to her figure. And she never left the house without a little mascara, even if it was the extent of her makeup routine.

Then she'd met Colton Ford. Suddenly she wanted to be feminine and pretty, especially after their disastrous first meeting when she smelled and looked like she'd fallen in a sewage tank.

Last week, she'd spent two hours watching YouTube videos to get step-by-step instructions in how to pin up her hair and apply makeup. This evening, she'd left the store an hour early to come home and get ready before she and Colt spent the evening trying to push her grandpa and his aunt together.

Piper knew tonight was all about getting the older couple together, but she couldn't help wishing she and Colt were going on a date. As she riffled through her clothes for the tenth time, she knew she needed to hurry or she'd run out of time to get dressed.

She yanked on a soft sweater the same shade of blue as her eyes, tugged on a pair of black leggings she'd ordered online in a panic on Monday when she thought about what she'd wear tonight, and pulled on a pair of knee-high black dress boots, also purchased online. Every pair of boots she owned came from the feed store and was either made for irrigating or cowboy boots.

With one eye on the clock, she used her curling iron to add a few well-placed curls to her thick, sometimes wild hair. After adding two additional coats of mascara to her eyelashes and a bit of blush to her cheeks, she spritzed on her favorite perfume. The scent reminded her of her mother and wonderful times they'd spent together when her mom had tried to teach her about being feminine.

Piper scrutinized her image as she stared into the long mirror hanging on the inside of her closet door. The outfit needed something and she wasn't sure what. A scarf? A necklace? Someone who knew what they were doing to wear it?

With a flash of inspiration, she opened a wooden jewelry box that had been her mother's. After a quick perusal of the contents, she pulled out a long silver chain with a filigreed heart dangling from the end. The necklace had belonged to her great-grandmother. Piper slipped it over her head and turned to look in the mirror. She smiled. The necklace looked perfect. She wondered if her grandfather would recognize it. If he did, it would please him to see her wearing the antique necklace.

Piper rushed into the kitchen and picked up a tissue paper-wrapped gift she was taking to Ruth, tucking it inside her purse. She'd just gathered her coat and gloves when she heard the doorbell chime.

Her grandfather never rang the bell, so she wondered what prompted him to do so this evening. Grabbing her things, she hurried to the front of the house, pulling on her coat as she went. She dropped her purse on a nearby table to have a free hand to open the door while she started to button her coat.

"Hey, Grandpa, I'm ready…" She glanced up and into Colton Ford's smiling face. Mercy! The man seemed to get more handsome every time she saw him. He'd stopped by the store on Tuesday to pick up a few supplies for the ranch. The sight of him then, dressed in a chore coat with a ratty ball cap on his head, made her mouth water.

But as he stood on her porch, one arm leaning against the door frame, with a black cowboy hat pushed back on his golden brown hair and a dark wool coat encasing his broad shoulders, he looked positively scrumptious.

Scrumptious? Piper had no idea where that word came from. Not once had it ever popped up in her vocabulary, but she had an idea it was generated by the attractive cowboy standing in front of her.

"Hi, Colt."

"Evening, Piper. Aunt Ruth called and said Rand decided it would be easier if I picked you up and he brought her to dinner. Hope you don't mind riding with me." He offered her an inviting smile that made her knees quiver.

"No. I don't mind at all. I'm ready to go." She picked up her purse and stepped outside.

Colt looked around, as though he expected one, or several, of her animals to greet him. "Where's the gang?" he asked in a teasing tone.

"Doogie was hanging out in the barn with the kittens last I saw him. By now, Simba has probably escaped and joined them."

"Better the barn than the pig's pen," Colt said, taking her elbow in his hand as they went down the porch steps and along the walk. "Does the goat get out often?"

"All the time. Short of confining him in a concrete box, I don't think there's anything I can do to keep him in his pen."

Colt chuckled. "I'd hate to see the little guy in solitary confinement. As long as he isn't hurting anything, I don't suppose it's a problem that he's out."

"Not really, although Moe, that's the pig, doesn't like him in his pen. That's why I was in there the other day when you came." Piper wished she hadn't brought that up. No doubt Colt would forever think of her as the dirty, smelly girl who walked around coated in muck.

He opened the pickup's passenger door and gave her a hand as she settled onto the seat. When he closed the door and walked around the front of the pickup, she took a deep breath, inhaling his masculine scent. One she was coming to like far too much.

She'd dated several guys since she'd moved to Holiday to take over managing the feed store. Normally, she went out a few times a month. But not a single one of the men she'd dated had caused her to feel as unsettled, excited, interested, fascinated, and nervous as she did around Colt. She had no idea what it was, exactly, about him that left her feeling like she was poised on the edge of the biggest adventure of her life. But something mysterious and wonderful, something uniquely Colton, certainly made her picture herself that way.

"Do you think Grandpa made any progress with your aunt this week?" Piper asked when Colt slid behind the wheel and started the pickup.

"She didn't say anything, but I took it as a good sign that she's letting him drive her to the restaurant." Colt smiled as he drove down the lane and turned onto the highway. "Is the Italian restaurant good?"

"The food is good and it's the nicest place in town," Piper said, wondering if she should have gone with her first instinct of wearing a dress. She didn't have many and she'd already worn her favorite last week. Most people in town thought dressed up was putting on a clean pair of jeans and knocking the manure off their boots, so she knew what she had on was more than appropriate to wear.

However, she got the idea her appearance last week surprised Colt. She wanted to see that look of appreciation on his face if he gave her more than a quick glance tonight. Realizing she'd once again allowed her focus to shift to the handsome cowboy beside her and away from the goal of getting Ruth to fall for her grandpa, Piper redirected her thoughts.

"I found a little something yesterday I thought your aunt might like to have," she said, watching Colt as he turned onto a side street that would take them to the restaurant.

"Oh? What's that?"

"A photo she must have given to Grandpa when they were in high school. It's of the two of them together, and it really is cute."

Colt glanced at her then back at the street. "I wonder what happened between the two of them. Do you suppose they broke up and that's what made him decide to leave? Or did his leaving cause the rift?"

"I have no idea and I'm pretty sure neither of them will tell us." Piper had tried to ask her grandfather a few questions, but he sidestepped each one of them until she gave up.

"I asked Fynlee if Matilda knew anything about it, and she didn't have any information either, if you can believe that. According to her, Aunt Ruth told Matilda it wasn't any of her concern and to not bring it up again."

"Ouch," Piper grimaced. "That must be a really sore subject," she said as Colt pulled into the parking lot at the restaurant. "Grandpa didn't say that in so many words, but he evaded my questions, too."

"A mystery full of romance and intrigue," Colt said in a theatrical voice that made Piper giggle.

She never giggled. In fact, she hated it when girls went around giggling at everything. It annoyed her to death.

What was this cowboy doing to her?

"I see them heading in. Ready to go?" Colt asked as he held a hand out to her.

Piper nodded and placed her hand in his. She'd been so lost in her thoughts, she hadn't even noticed him getting out of the pickup or opening her door.

He didn't release her hand, but kept their palms pressed together, his big fingers wrapped around hers as they walked inside the restaurant. Rand had just stepped up to the hostess station and Ruth was looking around.

"Hey, auntie, you look lovely as always," Colt

said, kissing Ruth's cheek.

Piper didn't know whether to be dismayed or inordinately pleased when he continued to hold her hand.

Rand grinned at her, cupped a hand on Ruth's elbow, and the four of them followed the hostess to a quiet table at the back of the restaurant.

"Will this be fine, sir?" the hostess asked.

"This is great. Thank you," Rand said, then helped Ruth remove her coat. Although she glowered at him, it seemed to lack the venom it held the previous week.

Piper looked at Colt. He raised an eyebrow and tilted his head toward his aunt. He'd obviously seen Ruth's reaction, too.

"Let me help," he said, moving behind her as she started to remove her coat. Unless she was dreaming, she was sure he intentionally brushed his fingers across her neck as he helped with her coat. She ignored the tingles that raced down her spine as he took her coat and hung it on a hook at the end of the booth.

Like last week, Piper sat down in the booth and slid over then Colt dropped down beside her. Ruth only frowned once before she slid into the booth on the other side. Rand took the seat next to her as a server brought them water and took their beverage orders.

"Cozy, isn't it?" Rand said as he leaned back and looked around. "I haven't been in here for a while. When was the last time we came, Piper?"

"I think it was for my birthday, back in September."

"That's right. We had that delicious chocolate cake for dessert. Hmm. I wonder if it's still available," Rand said, picking up the menu in front of him and opening it to the desserts. "And there it is. I might just have to get a piece of that later."

"They have the best house salad, too," Ruth said, opening her menu. "Matilda and I had lunch here before Christmas. I forget about coming here since it's a little out of the way."

Piper contemplated how anything could be too far out of the way in a town that only had two main streets and a half a dozen side streets where most of the businesses were located, but she kept her thoughts to herself.

She lifted the menu and studied the options, but she found it impossible to concentrate on food selections when Colt's rugged presence and alluring scent all but muddled her brain. Consumed with her thoughts of him and how glad she was to be sitting next to him at that particular moment, she jumped when his elbow bumped against her side.

"I didn't mean to startle you," he said, leaning close to her. His breath, warm and carrying a slight hint of mint, caressed her cheek. "Do you see anything you like?"

Yes! You! she thought, but managed to nod her head and point to an entrée on the menu. "I think I'll order the tortellini soup and a house salad." She turned to look at him, only then noticing the server ready to take their orders. "What about you?"

"The rigatoni with an extra sausage on the side sounds pretty good."

"I like the sound of that, too," Rand said from

across the table, smiling at their server.

The girl took Ruth's order and promised to return soon.

"I'm glad to see you wearing my mother's pendant, honey. It looks nice," Rand said, smiling at Piper.

She glanced down at the necklace she wore and nodded. "Thanks, Grandpa. I remember Mom wearing it. She always looked so elegant."

"And so do you, darling," Ruth said, giving her a warm smile.

"Thank you," Piper said, embarrassed by the attention, especially when she felt like an imposter playing dress up. Eager to change the subject, she looked from Rand to Ruth. "Is it true Matilda showed up at the President's Day party dressed like George Washington?"

Ruth laughed and leaned back in the seat. "Oh, my gracious! Tilly did wear that costume. She even had a tricorn hat."

"And she walked around spouting quotes from George Washington through the entire party," Rand said. "I think my favorite, though, was, 'It is better to offer no excuse than a bad one.' I'll have to remember that one."

"It sounds like she really added lively flair to the party," Colt said, looking at Piper. "Fynlee had some photos she showed me. Matilda really outdid herself with the costume."

"I wish I could have seen it," Piper said, envisioning the spectacle Matilda must have made. She loved that the woman did what she pleased and didn't care a bit what others might think about her.

Piper thought she could learn some valuable lessons from Matilda Dale. The woman had more chutzpah in her little finger than most people possessed in their entire body.

Piper glanced across the table at Ruth, noting her ladylike demeanor and gentle smiles. She could learn a few dozen from her as well. She pulled herself from her thoughts and tuned back into the conversation taking place at the table.

Colt asked Rand about an old building he'd noticed on the far end of town. Ruth and Rand discussed who used to own it. Ruth mentioned she and Matilda were working their matchmaking wiles on one of Justin James' friends and the granddaughter of the man who originally built the building.

Piper hoped Ruth and Matilda didn't get any bright ideas about setting her up with someone. Not that she minded going out on a date with one of the nice guys in town, but now that she'd met Colt, no one else held her interest.

Ruth and Matilda most likely wouldn't try setting her up with Colton. The women knew he planned to leave town at the end of the summer and Piper had no idea how long she'd remain in Holiday.

She glanced at her grandfather and wished for the millionth time he'd change his mind about selling the store and the farm. If he'd allow her to keep managing the store, she could perhaps cobble together enough money for a down payment on the farm. When he asked her to move into the house, he'd insisted she stay there for free, but she refused.

The last thing she wanted was to accept what she viewed as charity, even from her beloved grandfather. It made her feel marginally better when she wrote him a check for rent every month, even if he paid the utility bill. His argument was that he'd be paying it anyway since power was needed to keep everything from freezing during the winter and to keep the lawn and other landscaping alive during the summer.

The sound of a violin drew her from her thoughts as a high school student strolled among the tables, playing soft, classical music.

"Oh, that's lovely," Ruth said, leaning around Rand to watch the young girl play. "She's very good."

"She is," Piper agreed. The teen, dressed in a fancy gown, accepted tips from patrons as she stopped at tables and took requests.

When she came to their table, Rand whispered a request to her and the girl smiled. She began to play "When I Fall In Love."

Ruth's eyes welled with tears and Colt gave her a concerned look until Rand settled his arm around Ruth's shoulders and she leaned against him.

Piper held back a dozen questions. From the looks on the faces of the couple, it was obvious this song meant something to them, had been special to them at some point in their past.

As the last note faded away, both Colt and Rand gave the teen a tip and she went on to the next table.

"That was amazing," Piper said quietly. Afraid if she spoke up it would break the magical spell that had descended on their table, she smiled at her grandpa.

He nodded and scooted a little closer to Ruth. Much to her surprise, the older woman didn't try to pull away.

"I can't believe you remembered our song," Ruth said, looking up at Rand with affection.

"You don't really think I would have forgotten it do you," he said, smiling down at her.

Piper felt Colt's leg bump against hers then his hand took hers captive. The warmth of his skin against hers sent electrical sensations spiraling up her arm and down to her toes. She glanced over at him and he winked before he released her hand.

The server arrived with their food and the conversation turned to events planned in the community in the coming weeks and news from town. In spite of the delicious meals, they all ordered dessert.

"You have to try this," Colt said, holding up a flaky pastry horn stuffed with rich cream and dusted with powdered sugar.

She reached to take it from him, but he held it to her lips. Piper nibbled a bite, oblivious to the taste as she lost herself in the heat simmering in Colt's hazel eyes.

Piper licked her lips and she saw something in his gaze, like a fire flickering to life. He popped the rest of the small pastry in his mouth, then brushed his thumb along her bottom lip.

"You missed a little sugar," he said in a deep rumble.

Up until that moment, Piper had no idea the

human body could melt, but she was certain her flesh and bones were pooling beneath the table from the potent combination of his touch and the timbre of his voice.

Flustered beyond the ability to reason, she leaned toward him until her grandfather's foot connected with her shin. She glowered at Rand as she refocused her attention from Colt's lips to the busy restaurant around them.

Her grandfather gave her a knowing look. "So, Piper, what day did you say the spring chicks are arriving?"

Annoyed with her grandpa and embarrassed she'd almost kissed Colt in front of everyone, she scooted back and nodded her head. "They're supposed to arrive Monday. I plan to go in Sunday afternoon and get everything in place. Hailey and Ryan will clear out an area for the chicks Saturday afternoon at the back of the store by the tack supplies."

To throw the attention of those at their table off her and onto a different subject, she pulled the tissue-wrapped bundle from her purse and slid it over to Ruth. "I found this when I was doing some cleaning this week. I thought you might like to have it."

"What is it, sweetheart?" Ruth asked, picking it up and carefully removing the tissue.

"Oh. Oh, my!" Ruth said. Her initial surprise gave way to joy as she studied the framed photograph in her hands. "I remember that day so well."

Rand leaned over and studied the image she

held in her hands. "I do, too. A group of us had gone on a picnic. It was a few weeks before school returned to session our senior year. Do you remember? John and Marty brought their guitars and we had a sing-along."

"Yes, I remember," Ruth said. "You spent the day alternating between teasing me and trying to steal a kiss."

"Did he? Steal one?" Colt asked, grinning at his aunt.

Haughtily, she lifted her nose in the air. "I never kiss and tell."

"Well, Rand, you sly dog," Colt said with a chuckle.

Everyone laughed and Rand pointed to the image. He and Ruth stood together, arms entwined, as they gazed at each other in adoration.

"You were quite the dish back then, Ruthie," Rand said. "No one had dimples like you."

"Well, you weren't so bad yourself. There's a reason the girls all called you Dandy Rand." Ruth blushed, but leaned her head on his shoulder. "That was such a lovely day."

"Thank you for sharing this with us, honey," Rand said, glancing at Piper. "I'm sure if you keep digging, you'll find many of my old memories lingering at both the store and the house."

"I look forward to discovering them, Grandpa." Piper smiled at the older man as Colt squeezed her hand in his again.

"I better get back to the ranch. Carson has assured me we'll have a full and busy day tomorrow," Colt said, feigning a yawn, even though it was barely eight. “Rand, would you mind taking Aunt Ruth to Golden Skies? I’ll give Piper a ride home.”

“I’m happy to take Ruth anywhere she wants to go.” Rand never lifted his gaze from Ruth’s as he spoke.

“Great. Tonight is my treat,” Colt said, rising to his feet as the server arrived with the bill. In less than five minutes, Piper was walking across the parking lot with her hand wrapped around Colt’s arm.

When she gave him a curious glance, he grinned. “Since your grandpa and Aunt Ruth seem to have fallen under some sort of spell, I didn’t want it to break. I hope you don’t mind leaving a little early.”

“Not at all,” Piper said, pleased to see her grandfather making progress with the woman he clearly adored. “It’s a lovely night, isn’t it?”

Colt tipped his head back and looked up at the stars filling the sky. Although it was cool, it wasn’t the bone-chilling cold they’d experienced the previous week. The weather had been mild the last several days, and sunny, drying up the mud they had after the snow melted.

“It’s gorgeous,” he said, no longer studying the stars, but her.

Piper ducked her head at the intensity of his gaze and climbed into the pickup.

“Anywhere you want to go?” he asked as he drove through town.

“No. It’s probably good to call it a night. I need to be at the store bright and early tomorrow.

Saturdays are always busy." She looked out the window at the storefronts as they drove down Main Street.

"Carson has some horrible cleaning project planned for tomorrow, so I should probably be rested and ready for it, too."

"Horrible cleaning project? At the ranch?" Piper asked. Amused by the disgusted look on Colt's face, she got the idea he dreaded whatever his brother had planned.

Colt nodded. "Apparently, Uncle Bob never threw anything away he thought might be useful again, so all that junk is jam-packed into an old building behind the equipment shed. Carson decided we should clean it out and see if there is anything actually useful in there."

She grinned. "That sounds exactly like Grandpa. Except I have several generations of possessions to go through at both the house and the store. I'm glad they saved so many things, though. I love the antiques and the old photos. I even found some record books that belonged to my great-great-grandfather. I could tell you exactly how much he charged to shoe a horse or rent a carriage back when he operated the blacksmith shop and livery."

"Now that is awesome. Most of the stuff Carson pulled out of Uncle Bob's shed is along the lines of rusted out gas cans and broken tools."

Piper wrinkled her nose, thinking of the work awaiting Colt at the ranch. "Have fun with that project."

A derisive snort rolled out of him. "There won't be any fun to be had. Maybe I should just help you sort through stuff at the store. That sounds way more interesting."

"It is interesting and fun, partly because it's my family's history and partly because I love sorting through old things." She glanced at him then back out the window. "I don't get much time for digging into the past when the store is busy."

"Are you still planning to hire extra help?"

"Yes. I'm going to start advertising for help next week and hopefully have someone hired by mid-March if not sooner." She gave him a studying look. "Interested in applying?"

"Maybe. Depends on the hours and benefits."

"Oh, it's just part-time work, Colt. There are no benefits, or paid vacation, or anything like that."

He turned onto her lane. "That's not the type of benefit I meant."

Confused, she stared at him. "What other kind is there? Retirement accounts are definitely not on the table."

As soon as he parked the pickup, he jumped out, ran around to her door and opened it. He tossed his hat on the seat behind her, then bracketed her face with his hands. "This kind of benefit, pretty Piper."

His mouth took hers captive as he pressed his lips to hers in a sweet yet skillful kiss that left her seeing stars. He kissed her again, a soft brushing of the lips before he pulled back and held his hand out to her.

Fingers trembling, she placed her palm against his and allowed him to lead her through the gate, up the walk, and onto the porch.

"I sure had a nice time this evening." He leaned against a porch post as she unlocked the door and set her purse inside.

"I did, too. I'm so excited to see Grandpa making headway with your aunt." Piper shoved her hands in her coat pockets and turned to face him. "Do you think she'll ever admit she loves him?"

Colt shrugged. "Probably. Aunt Ruth isn't one to get in a hurry about making up her mind. She likes things to be her idea. The photo you gave her tonight, though, was a great step in the right direction. I think she and your grandfather have a whole lot of history together. The memories alone might be enough to nudge her forward."

"I hope so. I really do love your aunt and Grandpa…" Piper broke off when Colt pulled his phone from his pocket, tapped the screen a few times, and suddenly Nat King Cole started to sing "When I Fall in Love."

"May I have this dance?" Colt asked.

Piper nodded, caught up in something she'd never even dared imagine. Colt took her in his arms and proceeded to dance with her on the porch. They swayed to the music, slowly moving their feet from side to side, while the world fell away. Something inside her, something she never even knew existed, broke free. Although she couldn't explain it, she felt as though she'd suddenly blossomed inside, like she'd spent her entire existence in a dormant stage and suddenly burst to life.

Heart pounding, breath tight in her chest, she leaned into Colt, into an experience she never thought might happen in her lifetime. Tomboys didn't slow dance on porches in the moonlight. Did they?

Then again, maybe they did if their dance partner was a charming, good-looking cowboy who embodied the hero of every girlish dream she'd ever imagined.

Between the moonlight, the music, and the brawny man holding her so tenderly in his arms, Piper lost the ability to distinguish between reality and fantasy. Perhaps she'd wake up in her bed and realize this had been nothing more than an Italian food-induced dream.

When Colt bent his head down and pressed his cheek to hers, Piper had never known such bliss as she did in that extraordinary moment. Her senses filled with Colt. With the scent of him, the sound of him humming along to the song, the taste of his kisses, the feel of his arms around her, along with the warmth radiating from his big body pressed so deliciously close to hers, her senses buzzed. If she dared open her eyes, he was all she'd see. That rugged chin, sculpted lips, straight nose, and crooked smile. Maybe she'd focus on his hazel eyes, bright with humor or glimmering with interest.

Far sooner than she was ready, the song ended but Colt didn't let her go. He kept dancing as though the music still played. Piper certainly wasn't going to interrupt and suggest they find another song. For several long, decadent minutes they simply danced and held one another as their hearts connected.

Finally, Colt lifted his head, just enough to look

into her eyes and smile. "You are beautiful," he whispered.

"You're not so bad yourself," she said in a breathy voice she hardly recognized as her own.

His mouth claimed hers in a hungry kiss. It wasn't gentle like the kiss they shared earlier, but one that hinted at passion and promises. Lips parted, Colt requested something from her, something she willingly, eagerly gave as she made her own demands with an urgency that left her dizzy.

Piper stood on tiptoe and pressed closer to him, consumed by their ardent exchange. Nothing else in the world existed except Colt. Except how much she wanted their kisses to continue for the rest of forever.

Unfortunately, Doogie leaped up the steps and plowed right into them, knocking them off their feet.

Colt hit the porch with a thud as he fell down and Piper landed on top of him. Doogie took advantage of their prone positions, attempting to lap their faces with his enormous, slobbery tongue.

"Doogie! Down boy! Get down!" Piper was so disappointed that whatever had been happening between her and Colt had come to such an abrupt end she wanted to scream in frustration. But under no circumstances would she vent her annoyance on the dog. He was just excited to see his human had returned home.

"Doog. What a surprise to see you," Colt said sarcastically, slowly sitting up after Piper rolled off him and hopped to her feet.

The dog woofed and plopped his backside in

the middle of Colt's lap. To his credit Colt good-naturedly pet the dog on his massive side as he looked up at her and shook his head. The beginnings of a grin tilted the right corner of his mouth upward.

In spite of her frustration, she laughed as Colt pushed the dog off him. Doogie cocked his head, as though he tried to figure out what Colt intended to do. The cowboy scratched the dog behind his ears before he got to his feet.

"Ladies and gentleman, that concludes this evening's dance recital," Colt announced as though he stood in front of an auditorium filled with people. "Take a bow, Piper."

She linked their fingers together and bowed to the darkness in front of her house, barely avoiding Doogie's tongue as she straightened. A giggle escaped when she looked over to see Colt wiping his cheek and chin on a handkerchief.

"You'll have to work on your reflexes if you don't like Doogie slobbers."

"Good to know," he said, grinning at her as he stuffed the handkerchief in his pocket and moved with her to the door. "I had a great time with you tonight."

"I enjoyed it, too," she said, uncertain what to do now that their lips were no longer locked together. Her heart still raced and she found it hard to draw a deep breath, but she felt bereft without a pair of brawny arms wrapped around her. A glimpse at Colt made her think he also remained a bit unsettled. "See you at church Sunday?"

"I'll be there." He held the screen door open as

she pushed open the heavy wooden entry door and stepped inside. "Sweet dreams, pretty Piper."

"You, too, Colton. Good night." Quietly, she shut the door behind her and managed to make it to the couch before she collapsed with a happy sigh. Awake or dreaming, tonight with Colt was an evening she'd never, ever forget.

Chapter Seven

"Incoming!" Carson called as he tossed a box to Colt.

Colt jumped when the box bounced off his shoulder and landed on the floor of the storage shed with a thud, stirring up a cloud of dust that made him sneeze twice.

"Hey, watch it!" he scowled at his brother as he stood on a ladder on the other side of the shed.

"Pay attention, bro. I've asked you multiple questions since we've been out here, but you look like you are lost in space." Carson smirked as he pulled another box down from the loft. "What, or should I say who, is on your mind?"

Colt's scowl deepened. There was no way on earth he'd tell his brother he'd been so caught up in his thoughts of Piper and the life-altering kisses they'd shared the previous evening that he could hardly think straight. He'd kissed a lot of girls in his twenty-four years, but not one had ever affected him the way Piper had last night. No matter how hard he tried, he just couldn't stop thinking about her, about how right it felt to hold her and kiss her, to… He snapped his attention back to the present.

"I don't think that's any of your business, is it?" he growled at his brother, attempting to corral his thoughts.

"Probably not, but you know I'm gonna harass you anyway." Carson smiled and tossed another box to him. "I've been around Aunt Ruth and Grams too much. I think their matchmaking tendencies are starting to rub off. They might be getting to you, too, since you and Piper are working so hard to set up Aunt Ruth with Rand. From what you said at breakfast, it sounded like things went well last night."

Colt nodded and set the box he held outside on a tarp. Carson wanted to clear out the loft area, sort through the boxes, and get rid of the things they would never use, like splintered shovel handles or tools so rusty and broken they'd be lucky to get the guy who collected scrap metal to take them.

Two of Carson's ranch hands and Shane Pressley, Sage's younger brother who worked at the ranch on Saturdays, were opening the boxes and sorting the contents into piles.

Colt stepped back inside the shed and caught the box Carson tossed to him. "When Piper and I left, Aunt Ruth and Rand were strolling hand-in-hand down memory lane. "

Carson frowned. "You left her alone with Rand? Did you take her home?"

Colt handed the box to Shane then turned back to his brother. "No, I didn't take her home. It seemed stupid for me to drive Aunt Ruth to HPH when Rand had to drive there. Besides, isn't the whole point to get them to spend time together?"

"Yes, but she's our aunt. You can't just go off and leave her at the mercy of just anyone."

"Don't worry, mother hen," Colt said, catching another box. From the weight dragging down on his arms, it felt like it was loaded with bricks. "Rand is a gentleman and I trust him to take good care of our auntie. You should have seen her eyes light up when Rand asked the violinist to play their song."

"That is pretty romantic, if you're into that kind of thing," Carson said, grinning as he hefted another box to Colt. "I still can't believe they have a history together none of us knew about."

Colt bit back a grunt as he caught the heavy box. "Well, from what I could see, Aunt Ruth is very into that sort of thing and Rand Milton."

Carson pulled the last box from the loft and gave it to Colt before he climbed down the ladder and they went outside to help sort through the boxes.

It didn't take too long to go through everything

and establish piles to toss or keep. The toss pile was then divided into garbage, recycle, or donate. Colt thought a lot ended up in the toss pile, but he couldn't blame his brother for wanting to get rid of things he'd never use.

When they opened up a box to find it stuffed full of old newspapers, Carson started to throw it away, but Colt grabbed it from him and pulled out the top paper. It was from December 1941 and had detailed accounts of the bombing at Pearl Harbor.

"Wow! You can't throw these papers into the recycle bin, bro. This is a box full of history," Colt said, taking out papers with information about the war. One had a story about a young man named Beaumont who'd been killed in action. He held it out to Carson. "Do you think that's Uncle Bob's brother?"

Carson read the article and nodded. "He mentioned once that he lost an older brother in the war. Do you think we should give these to Aunt Ruth?"

Colt started to say yes, but changed his mind. Anything connected to Uncle Bob was just going to pull her away from Rand and that wasn't what she needed right now. "No, I don't, but I do think we should save them."

"Agreed." Carson moved the box back to the keep pile.

Fynlee arrived shortly before lunch with Carson's pickup full of plastic totes so the things they wanted to keep could be better preserved than in the cardboard boxes that rodents had gnawed on and dust had infiltrated.

After lunch, they went back to work, starting to clean the main level of the shed. They'd gone through about half of the contents when an odd smell made Colt wrinkle his nose.

"What is that hideous stench?" he asked as he moved a box and the entire shed filled with a decaying odor.

"Definitely something dead," Carson said, making his way over and around broken pieces of equipment and deteriorating boxes.

"I figured that much out all by myself, Mister Genius," Colt smarted off as he moved another box and unearthed a decaying corpse covered in fur.

"Ugh, that's awful," Carson said, turning so his nose was buried against his shoulder.

"Here," Colt said, handing Carson the box he held. He used a broken-off T-post to lift the body of what had been a skunk and carried it outside to the trash bin.

"Let's give the shed time to air out before we go back in," Carson said, dropping the box he held inside the door. "In fact, I've had about all the fun with this I want to today. It's close to quitting time anyway."

Colt glanced at his watch. If he took a quick shower and headed to town, maybe he could talk Piper into grabbing a pizza with him. If they were lucky, there might even be a decent movie playing at the lone theater in town. He liked the idea of cozying up to Piper in the back of a darkened theater.

The question would be if she was willing to let him get cozy with her.

Her reaction to his kisses last night made him think he wouldn't have to work too hard to convince her to go out with him. Unless he was grossly mistaken, Piper was as interested in him as he was in her.

Colt didn't want to think about what might happen when he decided where he wanted to spend his future, or her grandfather actually found a buyer for the farm and store. At this point he and Piper were just friends with the hint of possibly something more. He'd worry about what might come of their burgeoning friendship another day.

Today, he just wanted to hold her again and maybe steal a kiss, or six. He sure wouldn't mind dancing on her porch in the moonlight either.

If he was given to romantic fantasies, last night would have ranked right up at the top. A beautiful woman, a beautiful song, a beautiful night. At least it was until that darn dog knocked them down.

Then again, having Piper land on top of him wasn't all bad. Maybe he'd buy Doogie a doggie treat to express his thanks.

He sighed, thinking of how perfectly Piper fit in his arms, how she tasted like sugar and spice from their dinner, how the sound of her voice caused his heart to race so fast it felt like it might explode.

When a hand reached out and gave him a shove, making him take a fast step to the side to catch himself, he glared at Carson.

"What was that for?" he asked, scowling again.

"Shane asked twice if you'd mind giving him a ride home. I assume by that goofy look on your face you're going to head into town to see Piper as soon as humanly possible."

Colt didn't know if he should be more annoyed by the fact his brother knew him so well, or that Carson had announced his plans to the men gathered around them.

"Sure, kid. I'll give you a ride," Colt said, forcing himself to smile at the boy. "Give me twenty minutes and I'll be ready to go."

"Thanks. I'll text Sage to let her know she doesn't need to pick me up." Shane pulled his phone from his pocket and tapped out a message.

Colt turned from him, gave his brother a sour look, then headed toward the house. He went to his room, took a fast shower and shaved, then dressed in record time. He finger-combed his hair, slapped on a little aftershave, then hurried down the stairs.

Fynlee was in the kitchen, making a cup of tea, when he walked into the room.

"Heading somewhere?" she asked with a knowing smile.

Colt gave her a speculative glance, convinced his brother had been blabbing his big mouth. "I'm taking Shane home."

"Yep," she said, taking a seat at the table and leaning back to study him. "Tell Piper I said hello."

Colt narrowed his gaze at her, making her laugh as he grabbed his coat and rushed out the door. He was halfway to town before he realized he'd forgotten to put on his hat.

After he dropped Shane off at Justin and Sage's place, he circled back around and went to the feed store.

He parked the pickup, tried to remember if he'd brushed his teeth after he showered, then popped a piece of minty gum in his mouth. With a charming smile in place and thoughts of how much he wanted to kiss Piper again swirling through his head, he pushed open the door to the feed store. Chaos greeted him in the form of fuzzy chicks and squealing children.

Three little girls giggled and screeched as they ran up and down the aisles, chasing half-grown chicks while a handful of adults tried to herd what seemed like a thousand little chickens toward the back of the store.

Piper and her assistant manager, Jason, were catching birds and placing them in a big stock tank as fast as they could. Each time they disappeared down an aisle to capture more, a pair of rascally boys lifted the birds out and turned them free again.

Colt would have laughed at the scene, but Piper appeared near tears and Jason looked like he might implode.

Carefully stepping past chirping, bobbing blobs of yellow feathers, Colt headed for the two troublemakers turning birds loose with lightning speed.

He crossed his arms over his chest and widened his stance as he reached them, doing his best to look intimidating. "That's enough, boys. If you don't want to have to clean up every bit of bird poop in this store with a paperclip and spoon, you'll knock that off right now."

Eyes wide and full of fear, the boys nodded their heads so rapidly they knocked off the little cowboy hats they wore.

"Scoot!" Colt tipped his head toward the front of the store. The two little imps grabbed their hats and started to run off. The older of the two boys stopped, turned around, and handed Colt the chick he still held.

Colt took it from him and set it inside the stock tank where Piper had lined the bottom with pine shavings and had a heat lamp set up. Clearly, she was expecting much smaller chicks than those filling the store with a cacophony of peeps.

He turned around to catch some of the chicks and looked in surprised as three little rabbits hopped by. Two of them were dark brown, but one was a caramel color blended with splashes of white. It was about the cutest bunny he'd ever seen.

It took little effort to catch the two brown rabbits. He set them inside an empty stock tank until Piper could put them where she wanted them. The third little rabbit scurried away.

Colt rounded up a dozen more chicks then listened as one of the kids in the store screamed and started to cry. Before he could make his way to the other side of the store where the hysterics were rising in volume, he heard Jason release a pain-filled yelp.

He deposited the chicks he held in their temporary accommodations then turned to find out what was happening on the other end of the store when he saw the bunny that got away from him earlier heading his way. Soft and fuzzy with little pink ears and an adorable nose, the rabbit looked like what every child thought of when they envisioned an Easter bunny.

The rabbit hopped beneath a shelf filled with stock heaters before Colt could grab him. He'd just knelt on the floor and slid his hand beneath the shelf when Piper rushed toward him, hands full of chicks.

"Don't touch him. He bites!" she warned as she gently placed the chicks in their pen then dropped down beside him.

Colt had no idea if she spoke to him as she slowly slid her hand under the shelf. His mouth went dry when her backside wiggled back and forth just a foot in front of him as she stretched to capture the vampire bunny.

A pair of dark blue jeans hugged her alluring form and she wore a pink sweater that inched upward in the back as she reached for the rabbit, exposing a smooth expanse of pale skin above her waistband.

White noise blared with a deafening roar in his ears and his vision blurred. For a moment, he questioned if his eyes had crossed from staring at her so hard.

"I got him!" she said in triumph and pulled the rabbit out. She turned, sitting on the floor so close to him he could smell the scent of her shampoo blending with the enticing springtime fragrance that was all her. She smiled and that tiny little cleft in her chin popped out of hiding, making him want to kiss her in the worst way.

Moisture flooded his sawdust-dry mouth so unexpectedly he swiped his hand across his chin, afraid he might start to drool. The smart thing to do would have been to move back, get to his feet, and go home. But Colton Ford didn't always do the smartest thing, especially when it came to a beautiful woman.

He shifted so he sat with his shoulder and thigh brushing against Piper's as she cuddled the frightened rabbit. She assured the little escape artist that Jason wouldn't really turn him into a pair of fur-lined gloves.

"Is he the reason for the tears and yelling?" Colt asked in a quiet voice. Tentatively, he brushed his index finger over the bunny's head. Although it didn't attempt to bite him, it gave him the stink eye.

"Yes, he is. Have you seen two other rabbits on the loose?" Piper asked, getting to her feet in one graceful movement that left Colt sitting on the floor staring at her long legs.

"Rabbits?" he asked, thoroughly distracted by her. Last night, he'd struggled to form complete sentences when Piper had removed her coat to reveal a sweater that hugged her curves and perfectly matched her spectacular eyes. The vintage necklace she'd worn made it nearly impossible for him to keep his gaze from straying to her chest. A heavy, filigreed heart hung on a silver chain, nestled in a valley between two flawlessly rounded hills.

"Rabbits," Piper repeated.

He blinked twice and glanced up at her. She gave him an odd look as she continued cuddling the bunny. Still feeling off kilter, he stood and pointed to the stock tank where he'd trapped the rabbits.

"In there," he said, slowly regaining the ability to think and speak.

"Great! I'll add Brer Stoker then get back to

catching chicks," she said, tossing him a pleased smile as she hurried to set the blood-thirsty bunny in the temporary pen with his friends.

"Brer Stoker?" Colt muttered, followed by a chuckle. He watched Piper hurry down an aisle, then went back to chasing chicks. Only she would name an Easter bunny after a man who created a vampire legend.

Chapter Eight

Uncertain if it was cabin fever or spring arriving in a few weeks that drove people to her store, but whatever the reason, Piper and her employees could barely keep up with the steady flow of customers Saturday afternoon.

Piper was on top of a ladder lifting a doghouse down from a high shelf when the delivery guy arrived. The sound of chicks peeping filled the store as the deliveryman set a stack of ventilated crates on the floor near the cash register.

She nearly dropped the doghouse on the customer's head at the sound. Once the doghouse was settled on top of their cart, she rushed to the front of the store and gaped at box after box full of chicks.

Not only were there twice as many chickens as she'd ordered, but they were three-times as big as she'd expected and two days early to arrive. She'd planned to come in early Sunday afternoon when the store was closed to get a place ready for the chickens. It was then she noticed a box of rabbits. She certainly hadn't ordered them.

"Ryan, come help me for a minute," she said, grabbing the teen's arm as she hurried past him where he stocked shelves near the register.

Together, they carried a large stock tank into the back of the store near the tack supplies then covered the bottom with pine shavings. She added a heat lamp while Ryan got water and feed.

She told Ryan to carry the boxes of chicks back to the stock tank and she'd help him get the birds settled after she assisted several customers waiting in line where Jason ran one of two cash registers.

Ryan carried back all the chickens then returned to get the crate of rabbits. Only one fuzzy little critter bit his thumb, drawing blood. Caught off guard, the boy dropped the crate and the rabbits escaped.

A moment later, it looked like a sea of yellow flooded the store as chickens appeared everywhere. Piper and Jason exchanged wide-eyed stares then ran around the front counter, trying to keep any chicks from escaping out the front door while herding them toward the back.

The bunny with sharp teeth bit Jason and a little girl who picked it up by its ears. She couldn't blame the rabbit for biting the child at the rough treatment, but Jason was ready to make hasenpfeffer out of the bunny and his cohorts.

Although she hadn't caught them in the act, Piper thought two puckish boys who lingered around the stock tank were hindering the progress of capturing chicks more than helping. Honestly, if the parents with children running amuck in the store would take the youngsters home, it would have aided the efforts to contain the chickens and rabbits far more than anything else. In spite of her suggestion they might want to come back to shop another day, the three couples all seemed intent on staying. The mother of one of the three little girls squealing and racing around was so busy filming the whole thing on her phone, it was no wonder she ignored Piper's hints to leave.

Frustration pushed Piper to the brink of tears as she raced around trying to catch fuzzy yellow chickens. She had no idea when he arrived, but she rounded a corner with her arms full of squirming chicks and there was Colt. On his knees, chest flat to the floor, he reached beneath a shelf for the fierce bunny.

"Don't touch him. He bites!" she yelled. Colt jerked his hand back and stared at her as she deposited chickens in their makeshift pen. She noticed the little boys were nowhere to be seen and credited Colt with their disappearance. Maybe she could sic him on the other kids in the store and the chaos would dissipate by half.

By the time the rabbits and chicks were settled, the customers departed, and the door locked so no one else could enter, Piper was exhausted. All she wanted to do was curl up on the couch and sleep until next week.

Hailey and Ryan helped Colt clean the floors, which were dotted with calling cards from bunnies and birds. She and Jason worked together to hustle through the store's standard closing procedures then all five of them set the store to rights.

Colt seemed to know intuitively how she liked things done. From the corner of her eye, she watched him joke with Ryan and tease Hailey. He was the kind of guy who got along with everyone and never lacked for friends.

Piper was more of a loner. She always had been. Girls in school had found her odd because she preferred to be outside climbing trees or tossing a ball than playing dolls or dress up. In high school, the boys she'd been friends with decided she was strange because she didn't care about clothes and makeup. She preferred to hang out with them and talk about football scores or welding techniques than listen to girls gossip about boys.

So she did her own thing and did her best not to worry about what everyone else thought. But somewhere along the way, she felt like she'd forgotten all the lessons her mother had tried to teach her about how to socialize and play well with others. Not that Piper was a social outcast, but she sure felt like it sometimes.

With her employees staying to help her restore

order after what Ryan was referring to as chick-ageddon, she didn't feel alone. In fact, she felt like she was exactly where she belonged, especially when Colt looked at her and winked.

A smile, a wink, just the sound of Colton's voice sent her into such a tailspin she started to wonder what was wrong with her. She'd never been in love before, although she'd had a handful of crushes. She'd been out on plenty of dates, even if they always seemed more like two buddies getting together to shoot the breeze than a couple out for the evening. There'd even been a few men she'd dated for several weeks, trying to force herself into thinking there could be more to the relationship, but there never was. Eventually, she broke up with them all.

She couldn't help but wonder if the reason for that was because she'd been waiting for Colton Ford to walk into her life.

Even though she'd only met him a few weeks ago, she felt like she'd known him forever. It was almost as if there was a part of her soul that had instantly recognized him as belonging to her.

Which was crazy, wasn't it?

How could she have such deep, intense feelings for a man she'd just recently met? She didn't even know his favorite color or what kind of gum he preferred. Weren't those details things a person should know before they declared themselves in love?

When she looked up from straightening a shelf of boots and saw him watching her, her stomach fluttered. Heat mingled with longing and something she hesitated to identify in the depths of his hazel eyes. He offered her a grin that made the fluttering turn into a full-fledged flurry of nerves before he went back to straightening a table of jeans.

Unable to stay away from him, she made her way over to where he worked. “Who taught you how to fold clothes so neatly?” she asked, impressed with his skills.

He grinned as he folded another pair of jeans that had been tossed on the table. “My mother. She insisted all four of her boys know how to cook, clean, do laundry, and take care of ourselves. Evie Ford is a force to be reckoned with when she makes up her mind about something, so my dad let her heap domestic skills upon our heads.”

Piper laughed as she folded the last pair and added them to a stack of similarly-sized jeans. “Your mom is a smart woman. Those are great skills for anyone to have. Your future wife will someday be very grateful you know how to do those things.”

“Any suggestions on a woman who might want to fill that position?” Suggestively, Colt wiggled his eyebrow up and down.

Piper blushed and turned away from him before she did something completely stupid and crazy, like shout, “Me! Choose me!” or threw herself into his strong, capable, unbelievably muscled arms.

Colt’s mouth-watering fragrance, a blending of aromas that put her in mind of sunshine and leather, surrounded her as he moved behind her. A shiver trailed down her spine at the feel of his breath, warm and minty, as it caressed her sensitive skin and stirred the tendrils of hair near her ear that had escaped her ponytail.

"Do you have plans this evening?" he asked in a quiet rumble.

She glanced over her shoulder at him as she stepped away from him, away from temptation. She walked toward the back hallway. "No. None at all. After this chicken fiasco…"

"Chick-ageddon," he supplied.

She waved to Hailey and Ryan as they clocked out and left then turned to Colt with a grin. "After chick-ageddon and a blood-sucking bunny on the loose, I may never have plans again. I'm beat. Why?"

"Oh, well, I just wondered if you might want to grab a pizza or something, but I'm sure this afternoon was exhausting. Maybe I can get a rain check?" he asked with a hopeful look on his face.

"How about you pick up a pizza and bring it to my place?" she suggested, not wanting to tell him no. "I'll find a movie for us to watch."

"Great," he said, his smile broadening as he backed toward the employee exit. "I'll get the pizza and meet you there soon."

Before she could tell him what kind she wanted, he disappeared out the door.

"Is there anything else we need to do before we leave?" Jason asked as he set a bank bag on her desk then tugged on the coat he carried in his other hand.

"No. Go home. Enjoy the rest of your weekend. Thank you, Jason, for everything."

He nodded, looking as tired as she felt. "No

problem, Piper. I'll see you Tuesday, unless you need me to come in Monday to help with anything."

"Even if I did, I wouldn't call after today. Grandpa could fill in for an hour or two if necessary," she said, making a shooing motion toward the door. "Go home and make sure you keep that bite clean so it doesn't get infected."

"I will. Who would have thought a cute little bunny could be so brutal?"

She laughed as Jason waved and left. Piper checked on the chicks and bunnies one more time before she turned off the lights, made sure the doors were locked, and left.

When she arrived home, she flicked on the lights in the kitchen and living room, tugged on a pair of semi-clean coveralls, and ran out to take care of the evening chores.

Although she'd been dragging half an hour ago, the idea of spending the evening with Colt revitalized her. Had he come into town to ask her out for pizza or did he just happen to show up at the store when she needed him most?

If he'd come just to see her, maybe he'd been enjoying their time together, too.

She fed the pig and made sure he had water, placed feed and filled the water bucket in Simba's pen even though the goat was nowhere in sight. She fed Jam and scratched along his neck in all his favorite spots when he sauntered over to see her. When she tossed hay to Charlie over the fence of his pasture he trotted up and demanded attention.

Piper climbed onto the top pole of the fence and smiled as he nuzzled against her. She held still, fighting the urge to touch his soft muzzle. Instead, she let him show his affection. He turned his body parallel to the fence so he could lean against her leg. She reached down and rubbed his neck, withers, and back, then made her way along his neck again.

Charlie shifted and glanced behind her about the time a familiar scent tantalized her nose. She glanced over her shoulder as Colt stepped up to the fence.

"I thought I'd find you out here with the animals," he said, letting Charlie nuzzle against him. Since the day he'd trimmed Charlie's hooves, the horse hadn't shied away from Colt. He'd been back once to check on him, and it was clear then Charlie considered the cowboy his friend.

"I'd hoped to finish my chores before you arrived with dinner, but Charlie wanted a little attention and I still haven't located Simba."

"I saw your kooky goat on top of that little shed behind the house. Is that where you keep the lawnmower?" he asked, as though it was the most natural thing in the world for a goat to stare down at him from on top of a roof.

"Yes. It's where we keep all the garden tools and equipment," she said, giving Charlie one more pat before jumping off the fence. Colt looked slightly disappointed, like he'd planned to help her, but the last thing she needed was his touch turning her head to mush. She just wanted to finish feeding the animals so she could eat dinner, too. Breakfast was a distant memory and she'd skipped lunch.

"Would you mind feeding the kittens? Their feed bowl and water dish are just inside the barn door," she asked as she backed away from him in the direction of the garden shed."

"I'm happy to do that," Colt said, turning toward the barn. "Felix! Oscar! Here, kitties! Come say hello, you little odd couple!" he called as he walked that way.

Piper watched the kittens run out of the cat door she'd installed for them on the side of the barn and race around Colt's feet. He hunkered down and picked them both up, talking to them. Although he spoke low enough she couldn't hear the words, the rumbling resonance of his voice carried to her, making goose bumps dance across her skin.

She took a step back and almost tripped over the dog. Piper regained her balance then put her hands on either side of the canine's face and gave him a loving rub. "I'm in big trouble, Doogie."

He woofed softly, as though he agreed.

"Come on," she said, taking a step away from the dog and patting her leg. "Let's find that obnoxious goat."

Once Piper coaxed Simba off the top of the garden shed and back to his pen, she fed and watered Doogie then met Colt at the back door.

"I hope the pizza isn't ruined," she said as they walked inside the house. Colt toed off his boots while Piper kicked hers off then shrugged out of her coveralls. At least they'd kept her clothes clean. She hung them on a peg then hurried into the kitchen with Colt trailing behind her.

"This house is fantastic," he said, looking around with interest since he'd not yet been inside. "Old houses like this, especially when they've been cared for and maintained, are amazing."

"Thanks. I love this house. Even if it's old, it has a great floor plan and Grandpa put a lot of work into restoring it." Piper washed her hands and glanced at Colt as she dried them. "Would you like to see the rest of it?"

"Sure," he said, hurriedly washing his hands then following her as she led him through the kitchen to a hallway at the back of the house. The first room in which she turned on a light was the farm office. She thought it had probably been a bedroom or nursery at one point, but her grandfather had converted it to an office with a big mahogany desk in the center of the room and bookshelves lining one entire wall. The shelves were packed with books, antiques, and a few art pieces. She'd always been afraid to ask how much they cost.

"Your grandfather set this up?" Colt asked as he looked around the room. At her nod, he grinned. "Just kind of looks like him."

"It really does. If it wasn't dark out, you'd see there's a great view of the small horse pasture out the window." Piper waited for Colt to step back into the hall then flicked off the light and turned on the switch in the next room. There were two guest bedrooms, one of which had always been hers when she visited. The bed remained covered in the pink and lavender flowered quilt her grandmother had made for her the summer she was eleven. Matching curtains hung at the windows.

"Let me guess. This was your room," Colt said, picking up a framed photograph of a freckled-nose girl with her hair in pigtails, rips across both knees of her denim overalls, and a squirming dog in her arms.

Piper nodded, thinking of the day the photo was taken. She'd found the dog wandering down the road and brought him to the house. The poor thing was half-starved and she'd sat for hours with him while her grandfather called around to see if anyone had lost a dog. The next morning, a family showed up to claim him. A little boy, a few years younger than Piper, dropped to his knees and cried when the dog ran up to him and licked his face, obviously excited to be reunited with his people. That was the first animal Piper had rescued and made her decide to do whatever she could to help an animal in need.

"A rescue project of yours?" Colt asked, setting the picture back on the dresser.

"One of many," she said with a smile and walked out of the room. He followed her through the kitchen to the living room. From there, they stepped into a short hallway. The door at the end opened to a large linen closet. A door to the left opened to a coat closet while the door to the right gave entrance to the master suite.

When the house was originally constructed the master suite had been a ladies' parlor, summer kitchen, and library. But her grandfather had remodeled it about thirty years ago, creating a large bedroom with a private bath and expansive closet. When she was little, Piper thought the big bathtub was a swimming pool, but these days, she looked forward to rare moments when she could fill it and give her tired muscles a long soak.

"Wow! I feel like I've stepped back in time," Colt said, slowly looking around the room. "Family antiques?" he asked, reverently running his hand over the marble-topped dresser.

"Yep. I brought this set down from the attic. Grandpa took the furniture that was in here when he moved to the Golden Skies, but he said I could have any furniture I found in the attic.

"Did you paint the room, too?" he asked, pointing to the robin's egg blue wall behind the walnut sleigh bed.

She grinned. "Yes, I did. I liked the blue accent wall with the pale gray paint on the rest of the walls. I think it makes the furniture pop."

Colt gave her a long, studying glance. "For a tomboy, you sure seem to know a thing or two about decorating a house and setting up nice merchandise displays."

Piper shrugged. "My mom was one of the top interior decorators in Seattle before she…" Her words faded away and she swallowed down the emotion building in her throat. "She taught me a lot when she was still able to work."

"You've got a great eye," Colt said. She could see him taking in the big area rug on the hardwood floor, the soothing landscape painting on the wall, and the pale gray damask curtains at the windows. "What's in there?" He pointed to the bathroom door.

Piper flicked on the bathroom light, glad she always made her bed and picked up after herself in the morning. She might be a lot of things, but a slob was not one of them.

"What a tub!" Colt said, walking across the room to the deep garden tub. He glanced at the walk-in shower, double sinks, and big closets that flanked the bathroom door before he walked through the bedroom and back into the hall.

Piper led him to the living room then up a set of narrow stairs to two small bedrooms. Her grandmother had used one for sewing. The old machine still sat beneath a window. Piper could barely reattach a loose button, but she couldn't bear to move anything in the room because it all reminded her of her grandmother.

"This is grandpa's hunting room," she said, flicking the switch and moving back.

Colt whistled and looked at the taxidermied trophies of deer, elk, moose, and bison heads on the wall along with a mountain lion poised in a threatening pose. Glass cases protected old guns, knives, swords, and one even held old musket balls.

"Has Carson seen this?" Colt asked, leaning over a case to get a better view of the contents.

The view of his jeans, taut across his backside, made her feel lightheaded and she had to work to remember his question. "No, Carson and Fynlee haven't been up here."

Piper had to turn away from the sight of Colt and those jeans encasing his muscular legs and fine caboose. "Shall we go eat that pizza, now that it's probably stone cold?"

"You've got a microwave, don't you?" Colt asked as they made their way down the stairs and returned to the kitchen.

"Of course." Piper took two plates from a

cupboard along with two glasses.

"We can heat it up that way," he said, opening a large pizza box. "I should have asked what you liked, so I took a guess."

Piper stared at half a pizza covered in her favorite toppings of ground beef, extra bacon, pineapple and black olives. The other half of the pizza was all meat with salami, pepperoni, bacon, ham, beef, and sausage.

"It's perfect," she said, smiling at him as she held out a hand to him and he clasped it in his. "Would you ask a blessing on this meal you so kindly provided?"

Colt offered a brief but heartfelt prayer then Piper warmed two pieces of pizza and handed them to him before she warmed two for herself and poured them both drinks.

"Did you decide on a movie?" Colt asked as they settled onto the comfy couch in the living room.

"I haven't had a chance. Do you prefer a western, comic book-based action, or something sci-fi?"

"Anything is fine. I'm not too fond of chick-flicks, but I'll watch most anything, as long as it's good."

She grinned and turned on the television. While they ate pizza and relaxed, they watched an action film she'd seen once but Colt hadn't. He seemed to enjoy it and when it was over, he didn't appear to be in a hurry to leave.

"Want some dessert?" Piper asked as she picked up their empty plates and started toward the kitchen.

"What are my options?" Colt followed her, carrying their glasses.

"Ice cream, stale cookies, or sweetened cereal." She grinned at him over her shoulder as she set the plates in the dishwasher.

"What flavor of ice cream?" he asked.

"Several," Piper said, motioning for him to join her in front of the refrigerator. She pulled open the freezer section and pointed to a dozen small containers that held about a cup of frozen deliciousness in each one. "There was a sale at the store when it snowed. I guess no one likes ice cream when it's freezing outside."

He smirked. "But you obviously do." Colt grabbed a container of caramel cone while Piper chose mint chip.

She handed him a spoon, refilled their glasses, and they went back to the living room. "Want to watch another movie?"

"You bet," he said, licking his spoon then smiling at her.

Piper had an almost irresistible urge to kiss away the drop of ice cream melting on his bottom lip, but turned her attention to the television instead.

By the time the movie ended, it was late, but neither of them seemed ready to say good night.

Colt gathered his outerwear from the back entry and carried them to the front where he tugged on his boots but hesitated to slip on his coat.

"Thanks for all your help today," Piper said, wishing she had a reason for him to stay. She couldn't recall the last time she'd enjoyed an evening so much, even if they'd spent most of it watching movies. They didn't need to talk to feel a companionship, a friendship, that went far beyond the surface.

"It was my pleasure." Colt lingered at her doorway, coat held in his hands, as though he hated to put it on and go.

Without her consent, her feet carried her across the floor, closing the space between them until she stood close enough to see the tiny mole high on his left cheek.

Piper could have easily moved into the circle of his arms and remained there indefinitely, but she forced herself to take a step back, both mentally and physically. "I feel like I should pay you for everything you did at the store today. We'd still be chasing chicks and rabbits without your help."

"I was happy to lend a hand, Piper." He set his coat on the table by the door then edged closer, eyes twinkling with mischief. "Although payment might be good."

"Let me get the store checkbook. I don't have any cash on hand. I can pay you…"

Colt grabbed her hand when she turned to head to the kitchen and pulled her back around to face him. "The kind of payment I'm talking about isn't money, pretty Piper."

Unsure if he meant kisses or something else, she tried to gauge his intent.

Quite unexpectedly, his teasing smile morphed into a remorseful look. "Scratch that. I'm sorry. That didn't come out the way I meant it to."

He gently squeezed her hand then released it

and took a step back. "I wouldn't want you to get the idea I expect certain… um… favors or anything. I didn't mean that at all." A sigh rolled out of him and he shoved a hand through his hair. "Sometimes my big mouth gets me into trouble. I'm really sorry, Piper. No payment of any kind is necessary for today, or any day that I help you. My apologies."

"You can stop apologizing, Colton," she said, closing the distance between them again. "I'm glad to know you aren't the kind of guy who expects anything from a girl. I've dated boys like that and they aren't cool."

He nodded his head in agreement, although his gaze remained tangled with hers.

It was in situations like this Piper wished she had some idea about flirting, teasing, and acting all girlish, because she honestly had no clue.

Relying solely on instinct, she took another step closer to Colt and slid her hands up his arms, amazed by the strength there, then looped her fingers around the back of his neck.

His eyes held questions, but when she smiled, he relaxed and wrapped his hands around her waist, drawing her even closer.

"I had a nice evening with you," she said quietly, suddenly fixated on his mouth, particularly his full bottom lip. When he wasn't smiling or teasing, Colt could appear quite serious, even brooding.

But right now, with his hands stroking lazy circles across the back of her sweater, she thought he looked far too inviting and appealing. Far more so than she could resist.

"Colton," she breathed his name on a whisper.

His head dipped down and his mouth captured hers in a sweet, incredible kiss that made Piper wonder if her toes really would curl inside her socks. He tasted of pizza and ice cream and something rich and subtle that was entirely him. She found the flavor of his mouth intoxicating.

"Piper Peterson, you are…" He kissed her forehead. "Fun to be around." He kissed her right cheek. "Big-hearted." A kiss to her left cheek. "Intelligent." He kissed her nose and she giggled.

He moved back just enough their eyes could meet. What Piper saw made her heart skip a beat, then another. She was sure the longing, love, and hope there reflected what was in her own gaze.

He brushed his thumb over her bottom lip and smiled. "You are so beautiful, pretty Piper."

"Thank you," she said in a soft voice, wondering if her bones might disintegrate when he slid his hands along her neck and buried them in her hair, kissing her temple before his lips plundered hers in a heated, driven kiss.

Lost in a sea of yearning, the sound of bells made her picture herself walking down a flower-strewn aisle toward Colton. A spring wedding was what she'd dreamed of the few times she'd allowed herself the indulgence of thinking about marriage. Tulips and daffodils would spill out of baskets and hyacinths would scent the air.

The bells rang again and Colt jerked back from her. "Someone's at the door," he said, stepping away from her.

By the way his chest heaved and he worked to

catch his breath, she could only assume he was as disoriented as she felt.

She tugged on the hem of her sweater to straighten it then yanked open the door.

Only no one was there. She stuck her head out and received a slobbery lick from Doogie that went from her brow bone to her chin.

She rolled her eyes and glared at the dog. "Did you ring the bell, Doog?"

Doogie woofed, and turned around in a circle, as though he'd done something to deserve high praise.

"That dog," Colt grumbled as he shrugged into his coat and stepped outside. He rubbed a hand along Doogie's neck and gave him a few good scratches behind his ears. "At least you didn't knock us down this time."

"I'm…"

Colt kissed her flush on the lips, cutting off whatever she might have said. "I enjoyed pizza and a movie with you. Maybe we can do it again sometime soon."

"I'd like that," she said, fighting to face the reality that the evening she'd enjoyed so much was coming to an end. "See you at church tomorrow?"

"I'll be there. Just look for the guy sandwiched between two crazy old women."

Piper smiled and watched as he jogged down the walk and out to his pickup. With a dreamy sigh, she absently rubbed Doogie's head before returning inside the house, still thinking about wedding bells and tulips.

Chapter Nine

Colt stepped into the feed store on a sunny March morning and came to an immediate halt. Piper was bent over, arranging potted flowers in a display that oozed springtime. It wasn't the cheery flowers or Easter-hued gift items that drew his eye, but the girl who snared his interest.

He moved out of the way of the door, but stood and watched her for several moments, enjoying the view. She had on a peach-hued blouse softened by ruffles on the sleeves and a pair of faded blue jeans that fit her like a glove.

Since they'd been seeing each other the last month, he'd noticed she seemed to dress more and more feminine. He hoped it wasn't for his benefit. It didn't matter to him if she was in dirty coveralls, although he could do without the pig and goat smells, or a fancy party dress. She looked beautiful to him regardless of what she wore.

When she straightened and stepped back to survey her handiwork, he moved behind her and pressed a kiss to her neck.

"Pardon me, sir, but that sort of behavior is not encouraged here in the store. My boyfriend might find out and I'd be in big trouble." Piper's voice held a teasing lilt as she spoke.

Colt playfully swatted her bottom then spun her around and pulled her into a hug. "How are you today, pretty Piper?"

"I'm great, thank you. Is everything okay at the Flying B?" she asked, returning his hug then leaning back so she could better see his face. "I didn't expect to see you today."

"Clearly," he said, staring at her with reproach. "At least I found out you'll let just any yahoo walk in here and kiss you." He shook his head in feigned disgust. "Shame on you."

Her gorgeous blue eyes twinkled with humor. "You know you are the only one whose lips get within kissing distance of mine, Colton Ford. Besides, I knew it was you long before you said anything."

His brow furrowed in a true frown as he studied her. "How could you possibly know that?"

"Because I could smell you and feel you."

He gave her a confused look, then turned his nose toward his armpit and sniffed, making her laugh.

She smacked his arm, smiling widely. "You're such a dork. I wasn't implying you stink. I meant that I recognize your scent, the fragrance that's uniquely you."

"Oh? Is that so? And that whole feel you thing? What's that mean?" he asked, wrapping his arms around her again, loving the way she felt in his arms. If he wanted to admit it, he loved her. It seemed far too soon to be in love, but he was. He'd tried to tell himself he had a violent case of spring fever, but it was more than that.

For the first time in his life he was in love, truly and deeply in love. In addition, he thought what he felt for Piper might be something that didn't come along every day. It was the sort of love that created a happily ever after. When he looked at her, he could so easily picture his future with kids and sunset horseback rides, sipping lemonade on the porch, and walking hand in hand even when Piper's brown hair was gray and his had fallen out.

Subconsciously, his left hand rubbed over his head full of dark hair, as though he needed reassurance he wasn't on his way to being bald.

Two customers entered the store and gave them a curious glimpse before heading down the center aisle, causing Piper to move back although she gave Colt a warm smile. "What 'I feel you' means is that I can sense when you're near me, that's all."

Piper moved another step back and pointed to

the Easter display she'd been working on. "And I could see you in that mirror right there."

"You're a stinker." He grabbed her around the waist and tickled her sides, drawing out more laughter before she tugged free.

She took his hand in hers and led him over to the display. "What do you think?"

Colt looked around the merchandise she'd grouped together. There were potted tulips and daffodils from the greenhouse set up in the parking lot. Garden statuary of rabbits and squirrels were interspersed with bright green moss mats and shapes made of moss like mushrooms and fairy houses. Signs with spring sayings, Easter candy, wooden crates filled with candles and home décor, along with faux bird nests holding wooden eggs added color and depth to the display. He picked up an enamelware cup the exact shade as Piper's incredible blue eyes.

"I like this color," he said, noticing there was an entire set of enamelware that matched it with everything from bowls to canisters. Piper had included a few pink and white pieces, too, but they didn't catch his eye like the blue.

"Do you think Ruth might like one of the pink pieces?" she asked, picking up a pink enamel bowl. "We could plant pink tulips in it."

"She'd love it," Colt said, setting down the cup he held and walking around the rest of the display. Piper had placed an old wooden chair shaped like a heart on top of the biggest display table. White paint peeled off the back and legs, but gave it character. Seated on the chair was a vintage-looking stuffed rabbit as big as a kindergartener.

"Antique?" he asked.

She nodded. "Grandpa said he remembered it being old when he was a little boy. I found it wrapped in a sheet and stored in a box on a high shelf. If anyone tries to buy it, they are out of luck. And if someone tries to steal it, I'll shoot them."

He chuckled. "You should stick a sign on the chair that says, 'not for sale.' That might help."

"Good idea," she said, taking out her phone and tapping a note to herself.

Colt looked over garden accessories, hand tools, and flower pots that were in the display, along with cowboy boots, clothes in spring colors, and a few books about flowers. Galvanized trays and buckets held everything from seed packets to sparkly belts and jewelry. He reached out and touched a scale that looked like it might have come from the original feed store. Piper had arranged moss and wooden eggs in pale hues on it and a sprinkling of silk apple blossoms around it added to the appeal.

"You amaze me, Piper. One day you can be outside mucking out Moe's stinky pigpen and the next day you're in here creating displays that belong in some fancy-schmancy department store in a big city."

She blushed but smiled, pleased with his comment. "Thank you. I guess I learned a few things from my mom, that's all."

"More than a few," he said, picking up a piece of cone-shaped coiled metal that held a nest on top of it made of raffia with tiny, fragile-looking eggs tucked inside. "Is that a bedspring?"

"Yep. I found a box of them in the storage shed at home. I noticed there are a number of crafty things you can do with them. I made about a dozen of those," she said, pointing to two more of the springs with nests.

Colt gave her a surprised look. "You made that?"

At her nod, he put an arm around her shoulders and pulled her against his side. "You truly are talented, Piper. Mom is going to love meeting you. She's always wanted someone to do crafty stuff with her. Fynlee says it isn't her thing, although I think she's pretty good at it."

The mention of his mother made Piper stiffen. "Are you sure you want me to meet your folks when they come for Easter?"

"Absolutely sure. They're going to love you." *Almost as much as I do.*

Colt hadn't gotten around to figuring out the perfect moment to tell Piper how he felt about her. Not when they both were so unsettled about their futures. Piper would have to move and most likely give up her job when her grandfather found a buyer for the farm and the store. She mentioned moving back to the Seattle area to be closer to her dad and his growing family, but she sounded less than excited by the idea.

If he wasn't mistaken, Piper considered Holiday her home and didn't want to leave, but without the feed store to manage, he wasn't sure what she'd do for work. She had training as a veterinarian technician, but the local vet's office was already fully staffed. It was almost an hour's drive to the nearest town. It wasn't much bigger than Holiday and the road there was treacherous when the weather was bad, so commuting wasn't an option.

Colt had no more idea about his prospects than Piper did about hers. He loved being in Holiday, but he couldn't work for Carson indefinitely. Even though Carson appreciated his help, Colt knew half the time his brother didn't really need the assistance. He had a good crew already working for him. Colt had taken a few farrier jobs, but his heart really wasn't in it. He'd even helped at the feed store a few weekends, but he refused to take payment from Piper. Not when it was a pleasure just to be with her.

Until he decided where he wanted to spend his future, he didn't think it was fair to ask her to be a part of it. Although that was definitely what he wanted — a future with Piper.

Before he did something crazy like drop to one knee right there in the feed store, he kissed Piper's cheek and started walking down the center aisle with her beside him. "Do you have any chicks left?"

"Just the two I kept. The last little chicken found a home yesterday morning. I'm so glad," she said, sounding relieved. "I don't know how the supplier messed up the order so badly, sending twice the number of chicks I ordered and they were so much bigger than I'd expected. And then there was the surprise arrival of the rabbits. I'm happy they all found good homes, though."

"Speaking of rabbits, how is your cute little

finger-biter doing?" Colt couldn't believe it, but Piper kept the rabbit that would sooner draw blood than eat a carrot. She'd decided rather than calling him Brer Stoker, to go with Rambo. Either way, the bunny, all adorable on the outside and killer-instinct on the inside, was now a resident at Millcreek Acres.

"Rambo is doing well. He's befriended Oscar and Felix, which is good because the kittens would not appreciate his bites. Doogie still hasn't decided if he's friend or foe since he got the fang treatment."

Colt grinned. The day Piper took the rabbit and two little chicks home, the dog had come over to investigate the new arrivals. When he sniffed the bunny, Rambo sunk his teeth into one of the folds of skin beneath the dog's jaw. Doogie yelped and whined, and shook his head, then leaped onto Colt and cowered against him, scowling at the rabbit like it was possessed with a demon. Piper looked at Colt and the two of them had to fight back laughter as the enormous dog hovered on Colt's lap.

"How are the chicks doing?"

"Good. Simba has claimed them as his. It's quite something to see the goat leading a parade of two little chicks. Then the kittens follow Dixie Chick and Buttercup, and Rambo follows them."

Colt shook his head, envisioning the wacky animals Piper had collected. "At least Charlie, Jam, and Moe stay where they're supposed to."

"So far," she said, picking up a shopping list someone had dropped on the floor and straightening a rack of leather work gloves. She turned to Colt and smiled. "So what brought you in this morning? Did you need something?"

"Just to see you," he said, tugging her around the end of the aisle where they'd have a little privacy. He gave her a quick kiss, one that was playful, but also communicated his affection for her.

"You're sweet," she whispered against his neck as she wrapped her arms around him.

His blood zinged through his veins while his heartbeat accelerated. Now wasn't the time or place to let his feelings for her run wild, though. She had a business to manage and he had a list of errands he'd told Carson he'd handle.

"Do you have time for lunch today?" he asked, letting her go and stepping back. Out of self-preservation, he had to put a little distance between them.

"I do, but I promised Grandpa I'd eat lunch with him at HPH," she said, giving him a look filled with such longing, he nearly pulled her into his arms again.

"I told Aunt Ruth I'd drop by to visit her, maybe we could eat lunch there together." He smirked. "It would give your grandpa another reason to be near my aunt."

She smiled. "I'd like that, and I'm sure grandpa would, too. It seems like for every step forward he makes in his battle to win Ruth's heart, she takes two steps back. Does she really not care for him?"

"I don't think that's it," Colt said, taking Piper's hand in his and walking toward the front of the store. "I think she's afraid to open her heart to him, and that she's somehow betraying Uncle Bob."

"It's too bad, because she and Grandpa seem so good together." She released a wistful sigh. "I wonder what they were like as teenagers together."

"Probably trouble," Colt muttered, thinking about what he'd been like at seventeen. His aunt had been a beautiful girl with deep dimples and a sassy look about her. He could only imagine the boys that chased after her. And from the photos he'd seen of Rand, he was the kind of boy who made the girls all swoon, as Matilda would say.

"I'll see you in an hour for lunch at HPH," Piper said, glancing at the big clock on the wall above the entry door.

"You can count on it, pretty Piper." Colt kissed her cheek then hurried out of the store, wishing he knew the answers to the questions filling his head and how to stop the ache of uncertainty that burned in his heart.

Chapter Ten

"We've got to do something about those two, Ruthie," Matilda said as she and Ruth stood at the window of her apartment and watched Colt kiss Piper's cheek. He closed her pickup door and waved as she backed out of the parking space and drove away. He slid behind the wheel of his pickup and left, heading the opposite direction when he reached the street running past Golden Skies Retirement Village.

Ruth sighed and turned away from the window.

"I know we do, but I'm not sure what. As far as I know, they haven't even admitted they love each other, even if it's clear as a bell that they're in love."

"Maybe you and Rand should…"

Ruth glared at her friend. "Don't you start in with him again."

Matilda grinned. "You protest far too much anytime I mention handsome Rand. You're as blind as your nephew when it comes to love. Rand would marry you tomorrow if you'd just let him know you love him as much as he loves you."

Skin that was normally pale turned bright red as Ruth glared at her friend. "I don't love him!"

"Yes, you do." Matilda took two cups from her cupboard and made tea. She handed a cup to Ruth who was still red-faced and out-of-sorts. "From the information I've had to piece together since you're so tight-lipped about it, you were in love with Rand in high school and you're in love with him now. Why not just confess the truth and enjoy what time you have left on this earth with a man who adores you?"

"Because…"

Matilda grinned then took a sip of tea. "That's not a reason. Besides, you know as George Washington would say, it's better to offer no excuse than a bad one and when it comes to Rand, that's all you've got — bad excuses. Bob would approve of him, Ruthie. I know he would and you do, too. In fact, I'm sure they were probably friends since Bob did a lot of business at the feed store over the years. Just give yourself permission to follow your heart, no matter where it leads."

"Haven't I done enough, agreeing to suffer through dinners with Rand in an effort to get those two kids together?" Ruth glared at Matilda.

"I wouldn't exactly call it suffering, but you and Rand have been helpful. I don't think Piper and Colton have a clue that your Friday night dinners are specifically to get them to spend time together." Matilda smirked. "And if you and Rand happen to…"

Ruth practically snarled as she glowered at Matilda. "Not another word."

The two women quietly sipped their tea until a knock on the door startled Ruth so badly, she almost dropped the cup. Her fingers trembled as she set the cup on the table while Matilda answered the door. She scowled as Rand walked into Matilda's apartment.

He offered Ruth a polite nod of his head although the teasing smile on his face made him look like a mischievous boy.

"We just saw you a few minutes ago at lunch. What do you need?" Ruth asked in a tone that sounded like she'd run out of patience with his attempts to woo her.

"I need to know what you self-proclaimed matchmakers are going to do about Piper and Colton. Those two need a little nudge if they're going to fall in love." Rand expectantly looked from Matilda to Ruth. "I don't think finagling them into eating meals together is enough. We've got to up the ante."

"We were just discussing that very thing,"

Matilda said, motioning for Rand to take a seat on her sofa. "Tea?"

"No, thank you." Rand sat next to Ruth. She would have scooted away from him, but she was already pressed against the end of the sofa. "I know for a fact Piper is planning to be home this afternoon. What can we do to get Colton over there? I think they just need more time together. Generally, when they see each other there's always someone, like us, around."

"But they seem to enjoy the Friday night dinners we've started," Ruth said, giving Rand a confused glance.

"Someone's enjoying them beyond those two kids," Matilda muttered as she settled on the chair across from the sofa.

Rand grinned at her then turned back to Ruth. "They do enjoy them and it's been fun for us, too, but we need to do something more. Have they been out on any dates? Piper hasn't mentioned anything to me, but I do believe she considers Colton her boyfriend. Does that mean they're going steady or something else?"

Matilda leaned back and grinned. "I gave up trying to understand what anything means these days when Fynlee was falling for Carson."

"And look at the grand efforts we put into getting those two together," Rand said as they all thought of the fake fire they'd created to force Carson and Fynlee to speak to each other when they'd given up on love. "We need to come up with something like that for Piper and Colton."

"We could lock them in a closet together,"

Matilda suggested. "Or trap them in the store for the night. They'd at least have food and water if we did that."

Rand shook his head. "I like Colton, but I don't want to force that boy into a shotgun wedding which is what I'd do if they were locked into the store alone for the night. The way he looks at my granddaughter, I don't think I could trust him to behave for an entire night."

"Let's start with something small, something easily managed." Ruth glanced at Rand then Matilda. "Something that's in broad daylight."

"What do you have in mind?" Matilda asked.

"Well, what if we…"

Chapter Eleven

"Thanks. I appreciate you fixing this so quickly," Colt said as he dropped a heavy tire into the back of his pickup.

Carson had asked him to swing by the tire shop and see if they could fix a tire that continually lost air. It didn't take them long to find the leak and repair it.

"Let us know if Carson has any problem with the tire," the shop owner said, then returned inside the store.

Colt walked around the pickup and slid behind the wheel. He pulled Carson's to-do list from his pocket and glanced at all the errands he'd checked off. All that was left was a trip to the hardware store to pick up a few pieces of lumber then he could head back to the ranch.

He started the pickup and was waiting to pull onto the street when his cell phone rang. He glanced at the caller ID and saw it was his aunt.

"What's up auntie? Didn't I just see you an hour or so ago?" he teased.

"Colt! Please come to Millcreek Acres. It's Piper and… oh, the animals!" Ruth sounded hysterical as her voice cut in and out.

"What's wrong with Piper?" he asked, hitting the gas and turning onto the street.

"Hurry, Colt! Please." Static made it hard for him to hear Ruth. "Piper needs…" The line went dead.

Colt tossed the phone on the seat beside him as he sped across town and skidded through the turn onto the lane to Piper's house. At least he thought that was where he'd find her from his aunt's phone call.

Heart thudding in his ears and chest knotted with fear, he slammed on the brakes and bailed out of the pickup when he saw Piper on the porch.

The honking of a horn drew his gaze to Ruth and Rand as the two of them waved from Rand's car as he headed down the driveway. The smiles on their faces made him think he'd just been scammed by two octogenarians.

Residual waves of fear and anxiety rolled over

him, but he took a deep breath and looked at Piper. She sat in a patch of sunshine on the porch steps, sunlight shining off her dark hair and surrounding her in an almost ethereal glow. She held a banana in her fingers as Rambo stood with his two front feet on her leg, nibbling bites of his favorite treat. The kittens tumbled around behind her while two little chicks peeped at her feet. Doogie rested on the opposite side of her from the bunny with his big head on her lap.

The idyllic scene could have been painted on canvas and titled "Farm Girl."

He opened the gate to the yard and Simba raced between his legs, nearly knocking him off his feet as the goat ran out of the yard in the direction of the barn.

"Hey, Colt! What are you doing here?" Piper asked, glancing up at him with a welcoming smile.

Without saying a word, he marched down the walk, placed his hands on her shoulders and pulled her into his arms, engulfing her in a hug. The terror that something had happened to her had left him so rattled, he couldn't yet speak. He needed to reassure himself she was uninjured, she was real.

His hands moved up her back. Gently, he tugged out the band holding her hair in a ponytail and burrowed his hands into the soft tresses. With his cheek pressed to hers, he breathed in her fragrance, inhaled the sweetness of her spirit, and tried to calm himself.

When her arms wrapped around his waist and she hugged him without question, he knew he could never let her go.

He might have stayed on her porch steps holding her the rest of the day if the dog hadn't pushed between them and nearly knocked Colt backward in his enthusiasm to be seen.

Piper laughed and pulled away from him, reaching down to pick up Felix as the kitten attempted to climb her leg.

Colt settled his hand on Doogie's back and gave him a good scratch. This felt normal — right — like his world had been upside down and now it was back in its rightful place.

He stared at the happy woman standing in front of him with a fuzzy, ugly kitten cuddled against her neck. Rambo smooshed his banana against her foot while her yard full of crazy animals pranced around like they were participating in a talent show.

It all felt so good, so right.

"Aunt Ruth called and made it sound like you were drawing your last breath. I raced over here and…" Emotion welled in his throat at what he'd imagined, the unfathomable pain he'd experienced at the thought of anything happening to Piper.

"It's okay, Colt. I'm fine. Everything is fine," Piper said, placing her hand on his arm and kissing his cheek. "I wondered what Grandpa was up to when he said he wanted to show Ruth something in the house. I bet they called you from in there. It wasn't more than a few minutes after they went inside that they tossed a hasty goodbye my direction. They probably planned to escape before you could catch them in the midst of their shenanigans."

"Aunt Ruth, Rand, and Matilda did something

similar, although far more dramatic to Carson and Fynlee." Colt yanked off the ball cap he wore and ran a hand over his head. "Those three are nothing but trouble."

"And you wouldn't have them any other way," Piper said, setting Felix next to his brother then looping her hands around Colt's arm. "Since you're here anyway, let's go see Charlie. He thinks you come here solely to visit him and he'd be disappointed if you didn't say hello."

"Lead the way," Colt said. He followed her out to the horse pasture, realizing he'd follow her anywhere.

Hours later, after he'd helped Piper fix Simba's fence, trimmed Charlie's hooves, and played chase and fetch with Doogie, he and Piper went into town and got burgers for dinner. It was early when he took her home, with the excuse of needing to get ready for branding at the ranch the following day.

She walked with him out to the pickup, their fingers entwined, and kissed him so tenderly, he wondered if his heart had turned to syrup when he finally managed to let her go and climb behind the wheel.

"You'll come tomorrow, won't you?" he asked as he started the pickup.

"I'll be there," she said, then blew him a kiss. "Sweet dreams, Colton."

He waved and left before he turned around and refused to ever leave her again. Instead of heading to the ranch, he drove straight to Golden Skies. It was time he and Rand had a talk.

Chapter Twelve

Piper got out of her pickup and walked around to the passenger side where she opened the door and pulled out a pair of chaps. Leather the color of buckskin was accented with dark brown fringe, silver conchos, and stamped along the bottom with delicate pink flowers.

She'd been six when her grandfather started teaching her about cattle and horses on her summer visits to the farm. She just hoped she hadn't forgotten everything she'd learned over the years because it had been a while since she'd participated in a branding or roped a cow.

She settled a wide-brimmed flat-crowned cowboy hat on her head, tugged on a pair of leather gloves, and unloaded Jam from the horse trailer.

Before she could lead the horse toward the barn where everyone was gathered, her grandfather drove up and hurried out of his car. With a grin, she watched as he gallantly opened the passenger door and held out his hand to Ruth.

The woman took it and appeared to be pleased he continued to hold it a few seconds after he should have let it go. She wondered if her grandfather was finally making progress with Ruth. It was about time it happened.

Matilda bounded out the other passenger door and waved to her. "Piper, darling! You look fantastic!"

"Hi, honey!" Rand ducked beneath the brim of her hat and kissed her cheek. "Are you excited to help out today?"

"More nervous than excited," she said with stark honesty. "It's been a while since I've done this. I hope I haven't forgotten anything important."

"You certainly look the part of a ranch hand today, Piper. I love those chaps," Ruth said, pointing to the flowers on the front of the leather.

"Thanks. Dad got them for me for my seventeenth birthday." Piper rubbed a hand down the front of them. "I'm sure they'll be put to good use today."

"It's such a lovely day," Ruth said, tipping her head back to look at the sun shining in the brilliant blue sky. "It's been a lovely April, at least so far. I hope this nice weather continues. If it does, we should have a beautiful Easter."

"I hope the weather cooperates. Dad and Tina called last night to let me know they are planning to come for the weekend. It'll be nice to see them," Piper said, glancing back at her grandfather. She wondered if he'd pull up a chair at their table at Millcreek Acres for dinner or join Ruth here at the Flying B. Either way, she was looking forward to seeing her father and Tina. Her stepmom had listened a few weeks ago when Piper had called her and poured out her heart, revealing her feelings for Colt and seeking advice. Tina had told her not to worry about the future, but to embrace each day as it came and be grateful for whatever blessings it might bring. Sound advice, but Piper still struggled to follow it and not worry about what might happen with Colton down the road.

"You should bring your family and come here," Ruth said, smiling at Piper, drawing her from her thoughts. "It's seems silly for you to cook a big meal when we'll have plenty of food."

"Oh, we wouldn't want to impose," Piper said.

Rand smirked. "She might not want to, but I wouldn't mind at all. Will you save me a seat next to you, Ruthie?"

Ruth blushed, but nodded her head.

Matilda threw her arms wide, sending the dozen bracelets she wore colliding into each other in a discordant symphony. "Well, hallelujah! Hold on, Piper. I think the earth might be shifting on its axis if this old gal is finally giving Rand a second chance!"

Ruth scowled at Matilda and swatted her arm with the handkerchief she held in her hand. "Hush up, Tillie."

"Spring is a time for embracing change. Don't fight it!" Matilda grinned then sashayed through the gate and up the steps to the door.

Fynlee raced outside, hugged her grandmother, then bounded down the steps and hurried over to where Piper stood with Ruth and Rand. "I'm glad I caught you, Piper. I wanted to invite you and Rand for Easter dinner. I hope you'll join us."

"I just told Ruth that we appreciate the invitation, but my dad and his wife are coming and…"

"Bring them along," Fynlee said with a smile. "The more the merrier." The vibrant woman looped her arm around Ruth's shoulders and turned back to Rand with a fun-loving look. "I'm stealing your girlfriend for a while, Rand. Carson requested homemade strawberry danishes for the morning snack and Aunt Ruth has the recipe memorized."

Piper patted her grandfather on the back. "I bet if you offer to help, Matilda will insist you wear a frilly apron, but Fynlee will make sure you spend plenty of time cozied up to Ruth."

"Oh, you just hush," Rand said, tweaking her nose then giving Jam a fond pat on her neck. "If you're going to go play cowboy with the others you better scoot, honey."

"I'm going," she said, taking a few steps backward. "Have fun romancing Ruth, Grandpa!"

He scowled at her, but then offered a wink

before he sauntered down the walk and up the steps.

Piper took a deep breath then headed toward the gathering of cowboys. Some were drinking coffee. A few were saddling their horses. Carson stepped on a bale of hay to address the group but turned to speak to one of his ranch hands. Colt glanced up from where he talked to a neighboring rancher and caught sight of her. He waved, said something to the neighbor, then jogged toward her.

"Hey, pretty Piper! I'm so glad you came," he said, wrapping his arms around her and lifting her off her feet.

She laughed, caught off guard by his greeting and the feel of his hard muscles beneath the palms of her hands as she settled them on his upper arms. "That's some greeting," she said when he set her back on her feet.

"You look wonderful," he said. His gaze raked over her from hat to boots and back up again. He tugged on one of the two braids she wore. "You could pose for one of the western advertisements you hang up in your store."

"Hardly, but thank you for the compliment." She pushed her hat a little more securely down on her head. "So, what can I do to help or should I just stay out of the way and go back to the house?"

"No, we'll keep you busy out here. Besides, I want to show you off," Colt said, slipping his arm around her waist as they walked toward the group. Piper knew most everyone there from many of them doing business at the feed store. A few cowboys in attendance from Pendleton and one from Baker City were strangers to her, but Colt quickly introduced them.

Carson cleared his throat and thanked them all for coming then laid out his plans for the day. When he finished, Piper followed Colt to where he'd left his horse saddled and waiting.

"I haven't roped or attended a branding for a while," she said with warning as she rubbed a hand along the neck of a young horse he was training.

"It's okay, Piper. Just do what you feel comfortable with." Colt gave her an encouraging look as he tightened the cinch. "And stay close to me. That's important."

"Of course it is," she said with a grin.

"Ready to do this?" Colt asked, motioning for her to mount Jam.

She swung into the saddle and nodded. "As ready as I'm going to get."

Although Piper rode whenever she could, she hardly ever spent more than an hour in the saddle. Stretches might have been a good idea before she left the house that morning, considering all the time she'd spend in the saddle today. She hadn't given a thought to being so sore she might not be able to move tomorrow.

Six hours later, Piper groaned as she bent over to remove her spurs. When Carson's dog, Gus, whined and bumped against her, seeking attention, it was all she could do to muster the energy to pet the sweet canine.

"Gus, get down," Colt said, striding toward her with a bottle of water in one hand and a brown paper bag in the other.

With a stifled moan of pain, Piper straightened

and smiled at him. "Whatcha got there?"

"I thought you might need a drink. It got warm today, didn't it?"

"The weather is incredible. It could stay like this for the next month and I wouldn't complain," Piper said, accepting the bottle Colt held out to her and taking a long drink of the cold water. "I had fun. Thanks for inviting me."

"You can ride next to me anytime, cowgirl." Colt gave her a teasing smile. "Have you ever team roped? You'd be really good at it."

"No, and I don't plan to. Grandpa taught me to rope years ago, but I felt as rusty as that can of nails I found in the barn yesterday." Piper grinned at him. "But thank you. I really did enjoy myself."

A huge part of what she enjoyed was spending the day with Colt. She loved to be outside, loved to ride, and it had been wonderful to help with the branding. Although it was smelly, hard work, she'd enjoyed every minute of it. A bonus was working alongside the good-looking cowboy she loved. Just being near him made her days brighter and better.

She thought he felt the same way, but by unspoken agreement, they seemed to have decided to keep their feelings to themselves. Nothing would come of a relationship between the two of them. Not when they both would likely leave in a few months and head their separate ways. The only thing that could come of taking their relationship further would be heartache.

In truth, Piper knew she should never have moved past friendship with Colt, but everything just happened so quickly. One moment she was minding her own business and the next he was there, leaving her with the feeling nothing would ever be the same again.

She didn't think it would matter when he left her, whether it was tomorrow or a year from now, he was the man she knew she'd love forever. Perhaps that deep-seated devotion was hereditary.

Piper had no doubt in her mind that her grandfather had adored her grandmother. They'd been an affectionate, loving couple. But he'd never once looked at her the way he looked at Ruth. When he was with Colt's aunt, her grandfather looked and acted so much younger. She could envision him as a strapping young man, besotted with dimple-cheeked Ruth.

Because of watching the two of them, Piper knew what she felt for Colt would never go away. He would be her lifetime love, regardless of the opposite directions life would most likely take them.

Suddenly depressed by the idea of not seeing him again, never tasting his kisses, or feeling those big, brawny arms wrapped around her, she couldn't bear to be there. Rarely did she cry, but tears burned up the back of her throat and stung her eyes.

"I need to get going, Colton, but thanks again for today," she said, giving him a quick kiss on the cheek and hurrying into her pickup before he had a chance to do more than give her a puzzled glance.

With a fake smile plastered on her face, she waved at him and headed down the driveway. It wasn't until she reached the road that would take her home that the tears started to fall.

The next morning, she was sore in body and spirit. She considered staying home from church, but forced herself to go. Colton invited her to join him for lunch, but she turned him down, pleading a headache. Her head really did ache, just not nearly as much as her heart.

She ignored her grandfather's pleas for her to spend the afternoon with him at Golden Skies and returned home. She moved a table and chair into a sunny spot in the backyard, gathered her beloved pets around her and worked on a project for the store, hoping it would distract her maudlin thoughts.

Hailey had texted her Saturday afternoon to let her know they'd sold the last of the Easter items in the store. With no time to order more merchandise, Piper decided to make a few things to sell. As she sat wrapping plain wooden eggs with jute string then gluing on bits of lace, vintage buttons and little pieces of trim, she thought about her future. Hers and Colt's.

She knew he wanted to start a horse training and breeding facility, but lacked the funds to purchase an established place. He'd put out feelers with several realtors all over the region and was looking for a piece of property in his price range. He wanted to find somewhere he could build his business from the ground up.

Piper encouraged, even applauded, his goals and hoped he could see them become reality. As for her, she supposed she could move to a bigger town or city like Seattle and get a job at a vet clinic. However, even her love of animals didn't make her love the job. If she could make a wish, she'd keep the feed store and work there until she could pass it on to one of her kids or grandkids.

That was never going to happen though. Not when Colton held her heart. She'd rather spend her life alone than pretending she cared for someone else. As much as she loved him, it wouldn't be fair to anyone if she did that.

Overcome with doubts and worries, Piper covered her face with her hands and cried. She cried for the young girl who lost her mother far too soon. For the hard years she and her father had endured. The lonely years that stretched before her without Colt's love. She cried like she'd never before allowed herself to release her emotions.

She jumped when she felt something touch her arm and looked beside her. Doogie licked her cheek and placed his big head on her lap, staring at her with sad eyes. Simba pushed against her leg on the other side while two kittens, two little chickens, and a bunny all curled around her feet, offering their version of comfort and friendship.

Piper wiped her eyes on the backs of her hands and sniffled. "Thanks, guys," she said in a thin voice, sniffling again. "What would I do without you all?"

Doogie woofed, as though he reassured her she wouldn't have to find out.

Two days later, Piper was in a better mood and frame of mind as she put the finishing touches on updates to the display at the front of the store. She'd hauled several old milk cans up to the front, along with vintage wire baskets, and an old high-wheeled cultivator with weathered wooden handles. She was sure it must have belonged to her great-great-grandfather.

Stands with seed packets, birdhouses, potted plants, and a child-sized set of patio furniture completed the display. She'd just placed the jute-wrapped eggs she made in a big galvanized bucket when her cell phone rang.

Without checking the caller ID, she answered it.

"This is Piper."

"Honey, it's Grandpa. I hate to bother you, but can you please come help me?"

Piper wasn't sure if he and Ruth were working another matchmaking scheme or if he truly needed her assistance.

Wary, she swallowed back a sigh. "Grandpa, where are you?"

"I'm at the bank," he said. His voice sounded uncertain and somewhat distressed, like something had happened. "Can you please come right away? I really need your help."

"I'll be right there," Piper said, disconnecting the call. She ran through the store to the storage room where Jason inventoried a shipment that had arrived that morning.

"What's wrong?" he asked, taking a look at the worry on her face.

"Grandpa called. Something's wrong. I need to go see what happened and I'll be back as soon as I can."

"Take all the time you need. I can handle things until you get back. If it's an emergency and you need to stay with him, just let me know. I'll manage until Hailey and Ryan get here," Jason said, giving her an encouraging look. "I hope Rand's okay."

"I do, too." Piper raced down the hallway and grabbed her purse from the office on her way out the door. She hurried through town and pulled into the bank parking lot just five minutes later.

Although she'd half expected her grandfather to be waiting for her outside, she went inside to find him talking to one of the tellers who'd worked there as long as Piper could remember.

He certainly didn't appear to be in a state of distress, although he didn't greet her with a bright smile as he usually did when she stepped beside him.

"What's wrong, Grandpa?" she asked, placing a hand on his arm. As strangely as he was acting, she contemplated driving him straight to the doctor's office. The thought of him having dementia or something along those terrifying lines sent her heart sinking down to her feet. A world without Rand Milton in it, or without him able to recognize her, made her want to run screaming from the building.

Instead, she smiled at the man who'd always made her feel loved and welcomed. "What do you need help with?"

"I need a hundred dollars. I'll explain why in a minute. Would you mind, terribly, withdrawing it from your account, honey?"

"Okay," Piper said, taking her wallet out of her purse and handing the teller her bank card. "What's up? Do I need to take you to see Doctor Dawson? What did you eat for lunch today? Did something upset you? Are you feeling feverish?"

"I'm fine, Piper," Rand said. He watched as the teller handed Piper a crisp hundred-dollar bill and her bank card. Piper tried to give the money to Rand, but he shook his head. "Hang onto that for just a minute." He tipped his head to the teller. "Thank you, Francine."

"Anytime, Mr. Milton. Enjoy your day."

Piper gave the woman a puzzled glance before she followed her grandfather outside into the early afternoon sunshine.

"Please tell me what you're up to, Grandpa." Piper stared at her grandfather when he started walking toward the corner. "Where are you going?"

"In there," he said, pointing to a building on the opposite side of the street.

Piper's eyes widened. She took a few hurried steps to catch up to him. He grabbed her hand and pulled her across the street toward the title company office. Her head began to spin and she couldn't breathe. The only reason her grandfather would go there is if he'd sold the feed store, or the farm, or maybe both.

When they reached the sidewalk, she planted her feet and refused to take another step forward. Rand kept going until her weight dragged him back since he still held onto her hand.

"Come on, honey, we need to get in there. They're waiting." His encouraging look did nothing to dispel her concerns.

"Who is waiting, Grandpa? If this is your way of telling me I'm about to be homeless or jobless, you aren't doing a very good job of being reassuring." Piper felt dizzy and battled the need to sit down when her legs threatened to give way beneath her.

Rand cleared his throat and placed his hand on her back, gently urging her forward. "I did sell the farm and the store. The new owner of the farm is going to take such good care of it. I'm excited about the possibilities. And I adore the new owner of the store. Great things are coming. I can feel it."

Piper looked at her grandfather, at the joy and excitement in his face, but she felt none of it. Only disappointment and frustration. She'd hoped, with all her heart, he'd decide not to sell. Even if she never brought it up, she wished he'd see how much she'd love to take over the farm and the store. With what she'd saved, she could have made a down payment on one place or the other, then scraped by to make monthly payments.

Why had she been so afraid to discuss the possibilities with her grandpa? He would have worked with her to come up with a payment plan, she was sure of it.

However, it was much too late to think of what she should have done. She recalled what Matilda said the other day about spring being a time for embracing change. Since she couldn't fight what was already done, she might as well accept it with a modicum of grace.

"Why do you need the money from me, Grandpa? If you sold both places, shouldn't they be paying you?"

"You'll see, honey. Now, come on. We've kept them waiting long enough." Rand pulled open the door and a receptionist greeted them with a broad smile. Rand acknowledged her with a friendly hello then walked down a hallway lined with offices. At the last door, he turned the knob and pushed Piper inside.

A man Piper recognized as the owner of the title company stood and welcomed her with an outstretched hand.

"Miss Peterson. Nice to see you. Please have a seat," he said, motioning behind her.

Piper turned to sit down and sucked in a gasp as Colton Ford grinned at her.

"Hi, Piper," he said, moving next to her and kissing her cheek.

Dumbfounded, Piper looked from him to her grandfather to Mr. Williams. "I don't… what's… why are you here?" she asked Colt.

He chuckled and guided her into a chair, taking the one beside her and lacing their fingers together. "Mr. Williams and your grandfather will explain the particulars."

"Explain what?" she asked, perplexed and growing frustrated. How hard was it to give her a straight answer? And what in the world was Colt doing there? She knew he couldn't be the buyer. Could he? He'd told her the farm was exactly what he wanted for his horse business, but he didn't have near enough money saved to be able to purchase it.

"Would you like to discuss the farm or the store first, Rand?" Mr. Williams asked her grandfather.

"The farm," Rand said, taking a seat on the other side of Piper, then leaning around her to look at Colt.

"Colton approached me with a proposal I couldn't turn down. He'll take ownership of the farm on Easter."

"On Easter? But that's... you can't..." Piper didn't know whether to cry, scream, or use her purse to beat Colt over the head. How could he decide to buy the farm and not even tell her. He knew her family was coming for Easter. Would he really leave her homeless in two weeks, on such a special holiday?

"Let's give them a minute, shall we?" Rand stood. He and Mr. Williams quickly left the room, closing the door behind them.

"What are you doing?" Piper asked, glaring at Colt as she turned in her chair to face him.

Much to her surprise, he dropped to his knee and took her hand in his. Then he began kissing each one of her fingers. When he reached her pinky, he held it up and grinned.

"See this beautiful little finger right here?" He gazed at her with so much love in his eyes her stomach somersaulted and her pulse kicked into high gear. "I've been wrapped around it since the first day I walked around the corner of the barn and there you were in the pigpen, covered with muck and trying to hide while holding a squirming goat. You're in my thoughts all day, every day, pretty Piper. Truth be told, you're there at night, too, lingering in my dreams and my heart."

"But, Colton, what's..."

He silenced her with a sweet kiss then leaned back, taking a velvet box from his pocket. "When I told your grandfather what I wanted to do, he gave me this. It belonged to your grandmother and he thought you'd like to have it."

He opened the box and took out her grandmother's wedding ring. Slowly, he slid it on her left ring finger. It fit perfectly.

Piper looked from the ring to him, still uncertain, still not quite able to believe her dreams were about to come true. A thousand questions raced through her thoughts, but the one that stood out was pleading for Colt to tell her he loved her, that he'd never leave her.

"Piper, I realized the other day when your grandpa and Aunt Ruth made me think you were hurt, that I would die if something happened to you. We haven't said anything, haven't even tried to express in words how we feel about each other, but I know you love me. I can see it in your smile, hear it in your voice, and feel it in your touch. You love me and I love you, with all my heart, all that I am, all I hope to be. I can't get you out of my mind or heart, Piper, and I never want to try. What I want is a long, long life with you beside me. I want to wake up to your smile and go to sleep with you in my arms. I love you so much, Piper Marie Peterson. Would you please do me the great honor of becoming my wife? I may not be good at saying how I feel, but I promise to spend a lifetime showing you how much you are cherished and loved. You are the one for me, Piper, the only one, and I can't even picture a future without you beside me."

Everything in Piper wanted to shout "Yes!" but the practical side of her needed reassurance. "Did

Grandpa tell you the farm and me are a package deal? Do you have to take me to get the property? Is that what this is about?"

Colt's grin melted and he shook his head as he returned to the seat beside her. "No, Piper. One has nothing to do with the other."

He sighed and kissed her palm then cradled her hand between his. She absorbed his warmth, felt the calluses brushing against her skin. Colt was a hardworking, honest man. Not one who'd strike a deal and take on a wife just to get a piece of ground. Regardless, she needed to hear the details.

"Nothing?" she asked.

"Obviously, I've bungled this quite badly," he said, sighing again as he studied the ring on her finger. "I should have listened to Fynlee and taken you on a horseback ride with a sunset picnic."

A grin tickled the corners of her mouth. "That sounds lovely. Is that still an option?"

His head snapped up and he saw her smile. Visibly, he relaxed. "It's definitely an option. If you want me to spend the next fifty years coming up with creative proposals, I'll do it and ask you to marry me at least once a week. I'm sorry, Piper. Let me start at the beginning."

"Yes, do that," she said, biting back a smile at the earnest look on his face. "I'd like to hear the whole thing, from start to finish."

"When I left your house Friday, I went to see your grandfather to ask his permission to marry you and to find out how to get in touch with your dad to ask his permission, too. I called your father and asked if he'd please give his blessing. Before he would, he made me give the phone to your grandpa and grilled him for ten minutes about me, my family, my moral character — everything. He finally consented and said that he and Tina would come for Easter."

"I wondered what inspired their sudden plans to visit," she said as pieces of a puzzle began to fall into place. "That makes sense."

Colt nodded. "It wasn't until Sunday afternoon that your grandpa called and asked what I planned to do about a ring. He said he thought you'd prefer your grandmother's ring to any I might find in a store. We got to talking about my plans of starting the horse training and breeding program. He asked if I thought Millcreek Acres would be a good place to build that business and I told him it would be perfect, but I couldn't afford a property like that. He quoted me a price that I couldn't refuse. Turns out I had plenty to cover the down payment he had in mind. Your grandfather thought I should combine the proposal with sharing the news about buying the farm, and that's why we're here instead of on that picnic."

"So you asked permission from Dad and Grandpa to marry me without any intention of buying the farm?" Piper asked.

"That's right. If we'd had to rent a room at the Hokey Pokey Hotel and live there until we could find somewhere to call our own, I would have done it."

"Now that's true love," Piper said, looping her hands together behind Colt's neck. "But why all the cloak and dagger to get me here? I still don't know what Grandpa wants with my hundred dollars or who he sold the store to. He did sell it, didn't he?"

"He's in the process of selling it and he should be the one to tell you the details about it." Colt kissed her ring finger and gave her such a look of love Piper felt her limbs turn languid. She wondered if she might just melt into a puddle on the floor.

Colt dropped to his knee in front of her again, still holding her hand cradled in his. "Piper, in spite of this poorly executed proposal, I do love you with all my heart. I need you beside me for now and always. Would you please, please agree to be my bride?"

"I will, Colton. I love you so much," she said with love and joy filling her heart to overflowing. Colt stood and lifted her in his arms as their lips melded together in a gentle kiss full of promises for their future — a future together. The kiss started to deepen, but the door swung open, startling them, as Rand returned with Mr. Williams.

Piper blushed and Colt grinned as he set her on her feet.

"Are congratulations in order?" Rand asked, looking at Piper's hand.

She wiggled her ring finger. "Thank you, Grandpa. It means so much to have Grandma's ring."

"I know, honey," Rand said, giving her a hug. "Welcome to the family, young man. It's a pleasure to know you'll soon be my grandson." He shook Colt's hand before they all resumed their seats. "Now, let's talk about the store."

"Yes, tell me about the mysterious store buyer

and why you needed me to get money out of the bank." Piper took the hundred-dollar bill she'd shoved into her pocket and handed it to her grandfather.

"The papers please, Mr. Williams," Rand said, taking the money and tucking it into his shirt pocket.

The man slid a stack of papers across the desk, along with a pen. He looked at Piper with a twinkle in his eye.

"Grandpa?" Piper questioned, glancing at the papers then her grandfather.

"Piper, I know you love that store as much as anyone who's owned it, maybe even more. I want you to keep on making it a great place and a vital part of the Holiday community. You're too proud and stubborn to let me give it to you, so you've officially purchased the business for a hundred dollars. It's all there in the paperwork. All you have to do is sign on the dotted line."

"But, Grandpa! I can't take your store. I have money saved. I can put money down, make payments." She grasped Colt's hand in hers. "We'll work hard and…"

"No, Piper. You already work too hard. I want you to enjoy life, to bask in the joy of being young and loved by a fine man who has promised to always do his best for you. To give me and your father peace of mind, he's even signed a contract. If he should ever turn into a blithering idiot and take complete leave of his senses and divorce you, ownership of the farm, store, and all their contents, minus his horses and personal belongings, reverts solely to you." Rand placed his hand on her back. "You are my last living relative, honey. Everything will be yours someday, anyway, so you might as well take this gift I'm offering now. Let me enjoy seeing your joy. Let me cling to the hope you and Colton will give me some great-grandbabies to spoil. Please, Piper. Consider this an early wedding gift."

Tears rolled down her cheeks as she threw her arms around her grandfather and gave him a long hug. "Thank you, Grandpa. Thank you so much."

She turned and hugged Colt, never wanting to let go. And soon, she wouldn't have to. All her dreams were coming true just when she thought they were coming to an end. She'd get to stay in Holiday near her grandfather, live in the house she considered her home, own the store she enjoyed running, and marry the man she loved with every fiber of her being.

"So, when are you kids thinking you'll get married?" Mr. Williams asked as he notarized the paperwork after everything had been signed.

Piper squeezed Colt's hand and gazed into his handsome face. "How does an Easter wedding sound to you?"

"Perfect, pretty Piper," he said, kissing her fingers again. "Absolutely perfect."

Chapter Thirteen

"Everything is so beautiful," Piper said as she and Colt stood beneath an arch bedecked with pastel spring flowers in the courtyard at Golden Skies Retirement Village.

"Not nearly as beautiful as my bride," Colt whispered in her ear then kissed that spot on her neck that made a delicious shiver roll from her head to her toes. He grinned and wrapped his arms around her waist, pulling her against him.

Content, Piper sighed and relaxed as she rested

with her back pressed to his chest. "I can't believe Aunt Ruth, Matilda, Grandpa, and their friends pulled this all together on such short notice."

This was an amazing wedding and reception that was far more than Colt could have imagined happening with just two short weeks to plan for their Easter wedding.

They all attended a sunrise service together that morning then rushed to complete final wedding preparations. Fynlee, along with Piper's stepmom, had whisked her off to get ready.

Whatever they'd done was worth every minute of effort, because he'd never seen Piper look more beautiful. Her dark hair was piled on her head, but tendrils fell around her face, tantalizing him. She wore far more makeup than he'd ever seen on her face, but it looked good on her, drawing his attention to her incredible eyes and dazzling smile.

The wedding dress Fynlee had helped her find on a hasty shopping trip to Boise was perfect for her. He had no idea how to describe it, but the long sleeves made of lace, filmy fabric, and full skirt accented her slim waist, long neck, and amazing figure. She looked elegant and so beautiful.

He grinned as he thought about Piper carrying a basket filled with tulips and Rambo instead of a traditional bouquet. Hailey from the feed store had donned heavy gloves and taken the rabbit back to the farm after the wedding so he wouldn't bite anyone, but he looked cute in the basket when Piper walked down the aisle. The photographer had taken dozens of photos just of the basket with the rabbit, so he hoped at least one of them turned out. In spite of his tendency to be a vicious beast to everyone but Piper and him, Rambo had looked angelic and sweet as he sat among the tulips.

Piper had been so easy to please about all the wedding details, no one had the heart to tell her the rabbit should stay home. In spite of concerns, Rambo's inclusion turned out great. Other than the rabbit, when Fynlee, Sage, Matilda and Ruth had asked Piper about wedding plans, she told them all she wanted was to be married outside surrounded by spring flowers and pastel colors.

The women had delivered beyond anything he or Piper might have imagined. Colt glanced around the courtyard and still couldn't believe how good it looked. Pink, yellow, and peach tulips, cheerful daffodils, and fragrant pink and purple hyacinths filled baskets and vases all around the courtyard. A variety of Easter-themed decorations, like egg shells filled with violets and roses in pastel hues served as centerpieces. Some of the Golden Skies residents had even created a gingerbread village, decorated to look like Easter cottages with frosting flowers and pastel-hued gumdrops.

The food carried out the pastel tones, including a tiered tray full of cupcakes frosted in lilac, mint green, pale blue, baby pink, and buttery yellow. Chocolate rabbits, pastel colored candies, and miniature candy bars wrapped in paper printed with scenes from vintage Easter postcards were scattered across the tables.

Colt lightly squeezed Piper's waist and bent closer to her ear. "I think the folks here at the Hokey Pokey Hotel are getting quite good at decorating for weddings on short notice." He tipped his head to where Ruth blushed at something Rand whispered in her ear. "What I can't believe is the fact your grandpa finally talked Aunt Ruth into getting married. I'm glad we got to share our special day with them."

"I'm so glad she accepted his proposal and our offer to make it a double wedding," Piper said softly.

Ruth, who loved the same colors as Piper, had readily agreed to the wedding plans. Colt was sure his aunt had gone above and beyond in trying to make everything special for Piper in thanks for them sharing their wedding day with her and Rand.

"They look so happy," she said.

"They do. Almost as happy as I feel today." Colt kissed her neck again. "I can hardly believe you agreed to marry this lonesome ol' cowpoke."

Piper turned and slid her arms around the back of Colt's neck. "Thank you for marrying me, Colton Lucas Ford."

Love swelled in his heart until it felt so full, he thought it might burst. Despite his nerves getting the best of him during his attempt to propose when he rambled like an idiot, he'd somehow convinced Piper to marry him. When he'd asked permission to marry her, from Rand and her father, he'd envisioned proposing in a few weeks, after her dad and stepmom had a chance to meet him. But Rand had assured him dallying was only depriving him of spending time with the woman he loved.

The old gent was right. Thanks to him, here it was Easter afternoon, and he'd be going home with his beloved bride.

Home with Piper.

That thought made him smile and he hugged her closer against him. Never had he imagined, even in his wildest dreams, when Carson invited him to spend a few months at the ranch that he'd be the proud co-owner of a well-kept historic farm where he could start his horse training program, or the local feed store, since he and Piper agreed to be partners in everything, starting today. He definitely never dreamed he'd be married to the beautiful girl who stole his heart the first time he set eyes on her, even if she was covered in muck and mud.

"I love you, Mrs. Ford. You're so gorgeous, you take my breath away," he whispered in her ear.

She blushed and moved a step nearer. "You don't look so bad yourself, Colton. Truly, you're the most handsome man I've ever seen and I can't believe you're mine. That first day you saw me, when I was trying to wrangle Simba out of Moe's pen, I thought I'd just die. No girl, even a tomboy, wants to be seen like that, especially by a man who's thoroughly captivated her. Despite me looking like a disaster and smelling worse, you fell in love with me anyway."

"All it took was one look in those spectacular eyes of yours, Piper, and I was a goner." His thumb brushed along the line of her jaw. "I love you so much, baby. Thank you for trusting me with your heart."

"Of course," she said, smiling up at him. "My heart, my life, my all, because you're everything to me, Colton. Today and always."

"Piper." Her name came out on a soft rumble as he lowered his head to kiss her, but a slap on his shoulder jolted him back to the fact they were surrounded by wedding guests, many of whom were enjoying the sunshine with walkers or canes in hand.

"Congratulations, again," Carson said, giving Piper a hug. He released her and thumped Colt on the back a second time. "Fynlee and I couldn't be happier for you both."

"Thank you, Carson." Graciously, Piper smiled at him. "It's kind of funny if you think about it. You and Fynlee wed on Valentine's Day and now we've married on Easter. Maybe those two brothers of yours will find holiday brides, too."

Colt and Carson looked at each other and laughed.

"I wouldn't count on it," Carson said. Together, they watched as the oldest Ford brother accidentally spilled punch on one of Fynlee's good friends. Their younger brother sat on a chair pulled into a corner of the courtyard, playing with his phone and ignoring the rest of the world.

"You never know," Piper said, pointing to where Rand danced with Ruth.

"I'm so happy for our auntie, I could bust my buttons," Carson said, grinning as Rand spun Ruth around and pulled her into his arms. "I'm just glad Rand finally talked her into marrying him."

"Did they ever say where they planned to go on their honeymoon?" Fynlee asked as she stepped beside them.

"No, but I heard Grandpa on the phone with a

travel agent. I happened to see two plane tickets the other day. It looked like they plan to fly out of Boise, but I couldn't see where they were flying to," Piper said, smiling. "I think they are excited just to have some time alone."

"As they should be," Matilda said, wrapping her arms around Fynlee and Piper, pulling them both against her.

Colt grinned as she kissed their cheeks, leaving behind a smear of bright pink lipstick. For Matilda, she was dressed rather mundanely. She wore a hot pink suit with bright purple shoes and a white hat dripping with yellow and purple flowers.

"You should be happy your work has paid off, Grams," Fynlee said, smiling at her grandmother.

"I'm ecstatic, darling," Matilda said, tilting her chin up a notch. "It's not every day a matchmaker can attend a double wedding that she's brought about."

"What do you mean?" Piper asked. "I thought we were helping you get Rand and Ruth together."

Matilda laughed and hugged both girls again. "I did ask you and Colton to help get those two stubborn old coots together. What you don't know is that I asked them to help get you two equally stubborn young people to fall in love." The woman clapped her hands together excitedly, making the bracelets on her arms dance and jangle. "It was perfect! You all assumed you were part of the matchmaking scheme, which you were, but not like you thought."

Carson laughed. "That's priceless, Grams. You really are getting good at this."

"I know," she said smugly then pointed to where the oldest Ford brother helplessly tried to fix his spilled-punch faux pas. "Your brothers might be a lost cause, though."

Colt grinned. "I don't know, Matilda. Look how far we came in such a short time."

"Well, perhaps there's something I can do…" she wandered off in the direction of their technology-obsessed brother.

"They better run while they can," Carson said, slipping his arm around Fynlee's shoulder and kissing her temple as they all watched Matilda pull their younger brother onto the dance floor.

"Too late. No escaping now," Colt said, wrapping his arm around Piper's waist. "I can't believe Matilda played us all like that."

"I can," Piper said, smiling dreamily as Ruth and Rand danced by.

Colt thought his aunt looked at Rand like he'd hung the moon and stars just for her.

Just like he'd seen Piper looking at him. He prayed he lived up to such high regard. Above anything, he wanted Piper to know how much she was loved and treasured. He planned to spend a lifetime making sure she understood just how precious she was to him.

Fynlee smiled at him. "If you two want to sneak out of here, we'll take care of everything. I think it's wonderful you're taking a week's honeymoon in the woods. There's no chance of being bothered there and it's perfect for you two."

"Thank you. I think it's going to be great, especially since Colt's bringing along our horses to ride. He still owes me a sunset picnic," Piper said, offering him a teasing grin before she smiled at Fynlee and Carson.

Colt was glad she seemed to hold a true affection for his family. His mother had adored her and all three of his brothers seemed to think he'd found quite a catch with Piper.

"Are you sure you don't mind keeping an eye on things while we're gone?" Colt asked as he started sidling toward an exit with Piper. "You have to be careful to keep your fingers away from Rambo. Simba will get out, no matter how hard you try to keep him in, so just try to keep him from running off the place."

"We've got you covered. Go. Enjoy your honeymoon. We promise the store and all the animals will be well taken care of until you get back." Carson pointed toward the door that would take them inside a hallway and close to an exterior exit. "No one's looking, make a break for it."

Piper took Colt's hand and they escaped before anyone could waylay them. They hadn't wanted to leave in a flurry of rice or birdseed or whatever Matilda had planned to toss at them.

As soon as they stepped outside, Colt swept Piper into his arms and carried her toward his pickup which someone had festooned with streamers and tin cans.

"Guess we didn't fully escape their traditions," he said, grinning against her mouth as they kissed. She pulled open the passenger door.

When he set her on the seat, she giggled and pointed to her grandfather's car parked on the far side of the parking lot. "Looks like they got Grandpa, too."

"They sure did." Colt started to jog around the truck, but stopped when Rand and Ruth appeared outside, looking guilty as they attempted to sneak away.

He glanced at Piper and she grinned, hopping out of the pickup. Together, they hurried over to the older couple.

"Busted," Colt said as they walked up behind Ruth and Rand while the couple engaged in a tender kiss.

"Oh, my gracious!" Ruth gasped, spinning around so fast, the full skirt of her pink dress belled around her. "You nearly scared the living daylights out of me, Colton!"

"Sorry, auntie. My gorgeous bride and I were about to sneak off and saw you trying to do the same. Congratulations, again." Colt hugged Ruth and shook Rand's hand. "Take good care of Aunt Ruth. She's special to us."

"Not nearly as special as she is to me. I still can't quite believe this beautiful girl agreed to be my blushing bride." Rand draped his arm around Ruth's shoulders and gave her a gentle squeeze. "Are you leaving for your honeymoon now?"

"Yes. We'll swing by the house and change, pick up the horses and gear, and hit the road." Colt was glad the spot they were heading to was only an hour away. They'd be all set up long before it was dark. Piper didn't know it, but he'd rented a nice cabin and had it completely stocked with food so everything would be perfect when they arrived.

Carson had driven out to the cabin yesterday to make sure everything was ready.

"Have a lovely time, my darlings," Ruth said, hugging Colt then giving Piper a long hug. "Do you need any advice about, um… the honeymoon?"

Colt bit back a snort of laughter while Piper's face turned a deep shade of red. His hand encircled her waist as he drew her against him.

"I think we'll be fine, Aunt Ruth, but thanks for asking," he said, winking at his aunt. "Are you two flying out today?"

"In the morning. I'm taking Ruth to Florida for two weeks. We'll see then if we're ready to come back."

"Have a wonderful time, Grandpa," Piper said, giving the man a warm hug then hugging Ruth again. "Enjoy every minute of your trip and time together."

"We will, honey. You two kids have fun. Call us when you get back from the woods." Rand kissed Piper's cheek again then opened the car door and helped Ruth inside.

"We love you," Ruth said, waving her fingers at them before Rand shut her door.

"We love you both, too," Piper said, squeezing her grandfather's hand before she stepped back.

Colt and Piper watched the older couple drive away.

"They're so good together," Piper said, sounding wistful and delighted.

"They are. You know who else is good together?" Colt asked, sweeping Piper into his arms again.

"You and me," she said, pressing her lips to his, kissing him all the way back to his pickup.

He set her inside, ran around the pickup, and slid behind the wheel. He started the truck then took her hand in his and kissed Piper's fingers. "Let's get started on the beginning of our forever together."

"I like the sound of that, Colton." She smiled at him with love filling her eyes. "I love you so much."

"And I love you, pretty Piper. I have since the day we met and I will until the day we part." His hand tenderly caressed her cheek. "My forever is yours."

Recipe

This easy recipe might not be exactly what Ruth would make, but I think the gang in Holiday would approve.

Strawberry Cream-Cheese Danish
1 tube of refrigerated crescent dough (8 crescents)
1/2 cup whipped cream cheese
1/2 cup powdered sugar
1/3 cup strawberry jam
1 cup sliced fresh strawberries
¼ cup granulated sugar
1 tablespoon cornstarch
1/2 cup cream cheese frosting

Preheat oven to 350 degrees.

Slice berries, drain, and pat dry. Mix with granulated sugar and cornstarch, set aside about ten minutes, then stir.

Mix powdered sugar with cream cheese, set aside.

Line a baking sheet with foil or parchment and give it a quick coat of non-stick cooking spray.

Line the crescent rolls down the center of the baking sheet in two rows, using the straight side of the crescents to form the center line with the pointy ends hanging off the edges of the pan. (It should look like you have four sets of pennants placed back-to-back in your pan, overlapping ends.)

Spread cream cheese down the center of crescents, top with jam. Stir berries then spoon onto jam. Fold ends of crescents toward center, sealing edges by pressing together. It's okay if you leave a little "breathing" room here and there. Crimp the ends to seal.

Bake until crescent dough turns a rich golden brown and berry juice is bubbly – about 20 minutes.

Remove from oven and immediately drizzle with cream cheese frosting. It's easy to get a good drizzle if you warm the frosting for about 10-12 seconds in the microwave. Pour over the top of the Danish and serve while still warm.

Author's Note

I hope you enjoyed another adventure in Holiday with Matilda, Ruth, Rand, and, of course, Piper and Colton! Thanks for coming along for the ride.

When I was thinking about the characters and story for this book, I kept coming back around to Matilda tricking two couples into thinking they were helping her. One of the unsuspecting couples had to be Ruth and Rand. I've wanted them to get their happily ever after since I first introduced their characters in ***Valentine Bride***.

But I had to figure out who Ruth and Rand would think they were helping. That's when the idea of Rand's granddaughter popped into my head. And since we already knew Carson Ford from the ***Valentine Bride***, and he has three brothers, it seemed perfect for one of those brothers to become the hero in this story.

Colton was a great character to create. He's handsome, charming, and kind, I could easily picture him fitting into the pecking order of the Ford family. When the story begins, he's struggling to figure out what he wants to do with the rest of his life. The fact that he's unsettled and uncertain worked so well with the storyline. And he makes such an awesome hero for Piper.

Truly, I enjoyed developing Piper's character because she seems so simple to understand, but it isn't until we get to know her that we realize she's quite complex. The inspiration for her tomboy ways combined with "girlie" skills comes from my younger years. I was definitely a tomboy... until I wasn't. In my teen years, it was hard to find that balance between being mesmerized with fashion and flowers while enjoying working outside on the farm, often covered in muck and gunk.

I loved how caring Piper was, too, especially toward animals in need. Colt was also great with her animals. Not everyone would take on a blood-thirsty bunny.

The inspiration for Rambo actually came from Captain Cavedweller. I was discussing the animals I wanted to include in the story with him. When I mentioned a rabbit, he told me a story one of his friends shared with him about encountering an attack rabbit someone had in their yard. His friend bent down to pet it, because it was a cute and cuddly appearing bunny, but the owner rushed over, warning him it would bite.

As for the assortment of other animals, I had way too much fun incorporating them into the story. When I was thinking of a dog for Piper, I wanted one that was big enough it would give Colt reason to pause when he first met it. That's when I thought of the dog from the movie *Turner & Hooch*. A *Dogue de Bordeux*, or French mastiff, would be perfect. They're big, can be intimidating, slobber all over, and are awesome!

Then there were the baby chicks. Just the idea of Easter and spring always makes me think of new babies (calves are my favorite!), but little fuzzy yellow chicks come to mind, too! I thought how funny it would be if there were chicks everywhere. For that to happen, there needed to be a feed store so that's how Milton Feed & Seed came to be.

It was wonderful to picture what the store might look like and all the treasures stored there. I could so easily envision Piper finding a box here and a box there full of antiques and priceless family mementoes.

A feed store not too far from us has some neat displays and that inspired the idea for Piper's amazing displays that greet customers entering her grandfather's store.

I could just see Ruth and Matilda waltzing in to shop with Colt or Rand popping by to check on Piper.

It wasn't until I actually started writing the story, though, that I decided Ruth and Rand would have a history together no one else knew about. Anyone who might have remembered them dating in their younger years was gone, so it would have been simple for them to keep their past a secret. And because they had a past, one that ended with Ruth's heart being broken, it made sense why she was so adamant in resisting Rand now. But I'm glad he finally won her over.

If you enjoyed reading another Holiday Bride story, I hope you'll let me know if there are characters you'd like to see in future Holiday romances.

Also, if you'd like to see more of the visual elements that inspired the story, be sure to visit the Easter Bride board on Pinterest!

Thank you, again, for coming along on another book adventure! I hope we meet another time between the pages of a sweet romance.

Thank you for reading *Easter Bride* I hope you enjoyed Piper and Colton's story and meeting all the animals! If you have just a moment, would you please leave a review so other readers might discover this book? I'd so appreciate it!

If you haven't yet read them, check out the other books in the *Holiday Brides* series!

Also, if you haven't yet signed up for my newsletter, won't you consider subscribing? I send it out a few times a month, when I have new releases, sales, or news of freebies to share. Each month, you can enter a contest, get a new recipe to try, and discover news about upcoming events. When you sign up, you'll receive a free story. Don't wait. Sign up today!

And if newsletters aren't your thing, please follow me on BookBub. You'll receive notifications on pre-orders, new releases, and sale books!

Love at the 20-Yard Line — Haven Haggarty is woefully inept when it comes to men and matters of the heart. Successful in her job as an image consultant with a popular business, she wishes she could enjoy as much triumph in her dating efforts. When she falls hard for a handsome wide receiver, Haven realizes she needs to tackle her fears or miss the opportunity to experience once-in-a-lifetime love.

Brody Jackson lives and breathes football. As a wide receiver for a popular arena team, he's determined to make it back to the NFL. Cocky and confident, he doesn't have the time or energy to be bothered with a serious relationship until he's blindsided by a sweet, naive girl who breaks through his defenses. He has to decide if he'll let go of his dreams or fumble his chance to win Haven's heart.

Turn the page for an excerpt...

Love at the 20-Yard Line

Wide receiver Brody Jackson caught a pass and grinned. He spun the ball around in his big hands as he and his teammates warmed up before the first game of the season.

"Check out cougar town, dude," he said, inclining his head toward the stands as a group of middle-aged women dressed in too much makeup and not enough clothes sashayed toward their seats.

"Ripe for the picking, man. Just your type," Marcus Smith teased, smiling at Brody. The two of them were not only teammates, but also best friends.

"Hardly." Brody glanced around the bleacher seats, searching for a girl that would fill the role of his type.

He'd dated blondes, brunettes, and redheads. He'd charmed tall girls, skinny girls, short girls, and voluptuously curved girls. Smart, pretty, sassy, and brainless - he was sure he'd dated just about every type of girl out there, but it was all in fun.

Not one girl had ever reached beyond the surface and touched his heart.

Brody planned to keep it that way.

Women were a distraction he could ill afford in his quest to play football with the pros. Someday his dream of playing at the Super Bowl would come true.

His current gig, playing with a well-respected arena football team, took him a step closer to making his dream a reality.

"How about that one?" Marcus asked pointing

to a tiny redhead taking a seat in the sponsor section.

"Hmm. She's got potential," Brody said, not really interested in the girl. She looked so petite and fragile, he'd be afraid he might break something shaking her hand.

"Sure she does." Marcus chuckled, then stopped and pointed to a girl taking off her coat near the redhead. "Now, talk about high maintenance, there it is."

Brody glanced at the classy, polished girl who appeared as out of place at the game as he'd be at the symphony.

She wore a sleek black skirt and one of those sweater set things that looked all soft and expensive, even from across the field. Curly golden ringlets escaped from a bun at the back of her head and the glasses framing her eyes gave her a reserved air.

He couldn't see her hands, but Brody would bet money she had long, fake nails and a gaudy ring on her left hand.

Under the assumption she was probably someone's trophy wife, he looked away.

"You're such an idiot." Brody shook his head at Marcus. "I don't want any part of that."

Before they could further speculate on the dating material available at that night's game, the coach motioned them off the field.

Excited as the first game of the season rolled into high gear, Brody played hard, having a great time. He waited for the quarterback to throw him a pass, flexed his long fingers, and took a deep breath.

With one eye on the guy planning to block the pass and the other on the quarterback, Brody grinned when the football spun through the air his direction. Leaping up, the ball went into his hand as if he'd tugged it by a string. He hit the ground running.

Although a tackle was coming, he pushed himself to keep going then absorbed the impact as he hit the turf at the twenty-yard line. Thrilled by the number of yards he covered, he lifted his gaze and looked straight into the prettiest blue eyes he'd ever seen.

For a moment, he forgot everything around him as he gazed behind the glasses and saw warmth in the girl's eyes. She was the girl he and Marcus had joked about being high maintenance before the game started.

At this distance, a sweet innocence about her drew his attention. Something stirred deep within his heart, leaving him breathless.

When a hand clamped on his shoulder, he rolled over, coming up on his feet and tossing the ball to a referee. He smirked as his teammates slapped him on the back and Marcus lightly tapped twice on his helmet. It was their way of saying job well done.

The cheering crowd provided a shot of pure energy surging through Brody, driving him on as his team trounced their opponents.

Determined to keep thoughts of the blonde-haired girl with the soulful eyes from knocking him off his game, he continually found his gaze wandering her direction through the second quarter.

Glad for halftime and the opportunity to regroup, Brody blocked out the people around him and attempted to center his thoughts on winning the game.

"Dude, s'up with you?" Marcus asked as he bumped shoulders with Brody.

"Nothing, man. I'm cool." Brody took a drink from a bottle the water boy handed him. He tipped back his head and closed his eyes, letting the cool liquid slide down his throat. A pair of blue eyes immediately filled his vision so he opened his eyes and sat up straighter.

"You don't look cool, bro. Something going on you need to tell ol' Marcus about?" Marcus knew all of Brody's moods and he could tell his buddy tossed some idea around in his head. They were far ahead of the visiting team and unless something disastrous occurred between now and the end of the fourth quarter, he was confident they'd win the game.

By rights, Brody should be on top of the world and shouting it from the rooftops. Instead, he frowned with worry lines etched across his forehead.

"I'm fine, man, but thanks for asking. You better pay attention to Coach and look snappy about it because he's giving us the evil eye." Brody grinned at the coach and nodded his head, pretending to listen to the direction they received for the last half of the game.

Further conversation ended as they headed back out to the field. While he waited to go out to play, Brody turned his gaze into the stands, trying to steal a glimpse of the mystery girl. She sat in the sponsor seats section, so if he wanted, he could ask the sales manager about her.

That smacked too much of an interest Brody was determined he wouldn't admit to, though.

A quick glance over his shoulder confirmed she sat sandwiched between two hulking guys who looked like twins. One of them tried to shove a mini doughnut dripping with chocolate topping in her face while the other waved a tray of nachos in front of her.

She shook her head and pushed at both of their hands. The one with the doughnut touched it to her mouth, forcing her to take a bite. Brody stood mesmerized as her tongue came out to lick away a drop of chocolate lingering on the corner of her pink lips.

Her glare settled on the guy with the nachos then she laughed at the one with the doughnut. Her face transformed as dimples filled her cheeks and the serious lines softened. She took the doughnut and ate it, licking the sticky frosting from her fingers. Brody had the most insane desire to do the same thing.

"Dude, you gonna play or not?" Marcus slapped Brody's shoulder as the coach motioned him onto the field. Quickly grabbing his helmet, he gave himself a mental lecture about blocking out thoughts of the girl and focusing on the game.

Far ahead of the other team as the fourth quarter wound down, Brody stood waiting for the next play, doing his best to ignore the blonde sitting three rows up, two seats over, between the twin terrors. He wanted to beat the stuffing out of the guy who kept bumping her shoulder and trying to get her to share his drink.

When the man placed a hand on her arm and leaned closer to her ear, Brody clenched his fists to keep from climbing up the bleachers and knocking him unconscious.

Now the other one was saying something to her, but she seemed to like him, smiling at him with a look on her face that bordered on adoration. That particular twin turned to the redhead next to him and kissed her cheek.

Brody forcibly returned his attention to the game before he got involved in something that was none of his business. None at all.

He caught a pass seconds before the buzzer signaled the end of the game and ran to the end zone. The crowd went wild when he made the final touchdown.

The team shared a round of high-fives and congratulations. Brody returned to the bench and unearthed a pen, signing his name on the football. He removed his helmet and glanced up to see the girl who captivated his interest trying to put on her coat while one of the twins held the back of it against her seat. She had her arms in the sleeves, trapped by the big dolt.

Without giving it another thought, Brody jumped over the dasher boards surrounding the field. He ran up the steps and looked down at the girl and her friends.

"Hey, I thought you might like the ball from the last touchdown." He held it out to the blonde staring at him as if he was speaking in tongues.

Up close, her skin resembled smooth porcelain and her eyes glowed behind the frames of her glasses. Springy curls escaped the messy bun on the back of her head and Brody battled a nearly irresistible urge to reach out and see if the golden strands felt like silk.

She rose to her feet and he experienced a moment of pleasant surprise to see she was considerably taller than the tiny redhead who stood next to one of the look-alike brothers. A whiff of a soft, tantalizing fragrance that raised his temperature several notches assaulted him as he leaned forward.

Brody continued to hold the ball out toward her. She worked her hand out of her coat sleeve and took it in a tentative grasp, offering him a polite smile. Relief washed through him to see no wedding ring adorned her left hand and her nails were, in fact, short and unpainted.

"Thank you, Mr. Jackson," she said.

Brody felt inordinately pleased she at least knew his last name. "Call me Brody," he said, accepting the hand held out to him by the more obnoxious of the two brothers. The two men definitely bore a strong resemblance to each other, but he could see they weren't the same age as he originally thought.

"Congrats, man, that was a killer game. I'm Tom and this is my brother Hale."

'Thanks, man." Brody shook hands with the second brother and smiled at the redhead.

"There's a party starting in a while. You'd be

welcome to come as my guests," Brody offered, hoping for the chance to spend time with the blonde away from the field. If he had his way, he'd take her home instead of the Neanderthal duo.

"Please, Haven?" Tom asked, nudging her in the side with his elbow. "I promise we won't stay too late."

Although he hoped she would agree, the longing to punch her boyfriend returned with a vengeance. The guy treated her as if she was an annoying kid sister, not a beautiful woman who, for all appearances, seemed refined and very feminine.

He rolled her name around in his head. It suited her well, although he'd never heard of anyone named Haven.

Prepared to plead with her to go to the party, he looked into her face and could see fatigue around her eyes. He wouldn't pressure her to go, but he wouldn't let her leave without learning her full name. If he was so inclined, he wanted to know how to get in touch with her.

"What's your name?" Brody mustered up his most charming smile. He'd been told when he used it women practically fell at his feet, ready to do his bidding.

"Haven Haggarty." Haven wondered why this particular player decided to bring her an autographed football and invite them to a party. Maybe it was something each player did for a corporate sponsor.

Despite the dull roaring of her headache, she was vividly aware of the very cute Brody Jackson out on the field. She'd watched him play with interest and noticed him gazing into the stands their direction but had no idea he was remotely aware of her or her brothers. Abby was a dazzling little beauty. Maybe she'd caught his eye.

In his uniform, Brody appeared incredibly tall and sinfully handsome. His jet-black hair was tousled and sweaty, but thick. His chiseled jaw ended with a firm, ridiculously square chin. Sensuously full lips and dark brown eyes added to his appeal, as did his deep voice, laced with a hint of gravel.

The symmetry of his face was perfect for modeling and she wondered if he'd ever considered posing for an ad campaign. She was always in need of good models for their clients.

When he flashed that megawatt smile her direction, Haven found it difficult to swallow, let alone speak. After barely managing to push her name past her lips, she frantically tried to engage her brain. He'd scrambled it with both his presence and that husky voice.

His large hand engulfed hers and an immediate stream of sparks licked up her arm, exploding inside her head.

"It's nice to meet you, Haven Haggarty." Brody attempted to gauge her reaction to him. Other than her eyes growing a little wider, she looked calm, cool, and collected. And ready to go home. "Maybe you'll come to the party another time."

She shifted the football he'd handed her beneath her arm and stared at him, unaware of the look passing between her two brothers.

"Maybe next time," Haven finally said, pulling

her hand from Brody's. She'd never seen such long, capable fingers. Hurriedly handing Tom the football, she dug in her bag and pulled out a small case. She removed a business card and handed it to Brody.

"If you ever want to consider doing some modeling, I'm always looking for a handsome face like yours." Haven blushed as the words left her lips. She sounded like one of the ditzy flirts who enjoyed the attentions of men like Brody Jackson.

"So, you think I'm handsome," Brody teased, waggling expressive eyebrows her direction, noting Haven's flushed cheeks.

Rather than respond, she finished putting on her coat. She shoved the football into her big bag and pushed against Tom's side, trying to get him to step into the aisle and go up the steps so they could leave.

"Thank you for the ball, Mr. Jackson, and congratulations on your victory." Haven gave him a smile that had lost most of its warmth before turning to follow Tom out of the stands.

Brody glanced at the crisp white card in his hand and smiled. He might not see Miss Haven Haggarty later tonight, but he'd definitely see her again.

Available now!

Hopeless romantic Shanna Hatfield spent ten years as a newspaper journalist before moving into the field of marketing and public relations. Sharing the romantic stories she dreams up in her head is a perfect outlet for her love of writing, reading, and creativity. She and her husband, lovingly referred to as Captain Cavedweller, reside in the Pacific Northwest.

Shanna loves to hear from readers. Connect with her online:

Blog: shannahatfield.com
Facebook: Shanna Hatfield's Page
Shanna Hatfield's Hopeless Romantics Group
Pinterest: Shanna Hatfield
Email: shanna@shannahatfield.com

Made in the USA
Middletown, DE
28 March 2019